Tapestry of Words

Published by Purple Unicorn Media

Copyright © 2023 The Caféists
Cover illustration by Robin Stacey

All rights are reserved.
No part of this publication may be reproduced, stored in a retrieval system or transmitted in any form or by any means, electronic, mechanical, photocopying, recording or otherwise, without prior permission of the publisher.

ISBN 978-1-910718-65-0

PURPLE UNICORN MEDIA

Gill Bazovsky was invited to take over and run this group over 20 years ago and inspired many members to write, start university courses and to be published.

Her continued passion for writing lives on in the pages. Enjoy, be inspired....CREATE!

With special thanks to all contributors, especially Marilyn Morgan for initiating the group.

Table of Contents

Gill Bazovsky
Happiness in Solitude 9
Memories of Bluebells in the Churnet Valley (below Alton Towers) 11

Margaret Bevan
Poetic Injustice 14
Derailed 20
Just the job 21
Arrivederci Rhondda 26

Judith Blakemore
Jasmine Floral Arch 39
Tiffany Lamp at 11 o'clock 40
Ship on a Ledge 41
Steve Ferris in composition 42

Ken Blakemore
Love Duet 44
The Accompanier 46

Joey Clarke
Bluefields 49

Steve Cound
A Tale of Penllergaer Woods 59
Death Ray Matthews 65
Liminality 74

My Metaphysical Poem 82
Prose Poetry; Caswell 85
Zed's Head 87
A Trumpeter Swan greets his mate on a lake in Hickory Corners, Michigan 91

Geraldine Edwards
A Bygone Street Remembered 93

Steve Ferris
The Hazel Tree (Dappled Light) 106
The Fragile Earth 110
Downstream, The Crossroads 112
A Journey or Just a Dream 115
Greed and Beliefs 119

Frances Susan Gardner
Mystic's Cavern Corner 121
Cock-A-Loo 122
Trick of the Moon 123
Mr Peck 124
You Can Keep your Hat on 125

Jane Harrison
Garden Flowers on Easel 127
Marooned Shell 128
Still Life Composition 129

M.B.Howells
   A last minute holiday to Sri Lanka................131
Anne Marie
   Giraffes in Love 134
Annette Nash
   Unsung Hero 136
Claire Rozario
   Good Morning World 139
   My Feathered Friend 140
   Night Train 146
   The Tailor and the Thief 151
   The Edge of Life 160
   The Dawn of the Rats 161
   Yungblud 165
Gina Smith
   Storm on the Horizon 167
Mike Witchell
   Glyde 169
   What's Sauce for the Goose 173
   Ladder 177
   Leaves 181
   Mangle 185
   Pants 189

Gill

Bazovsky

'Gill Bazovsky' by Claire Rozario
Acrylic on canvas.

HAPPINESS IN SOLITUDE

From my place
I look out over rooftops of grey slate,
And see black ships on the far horizon;
Across the wide bay of the world,
Arched by a fading rainbow.

Turning
I am drawn into the crimson glow,
And dim shadows of my Edwardian room.
I look in my oval glass and gather
Reflections of happiness.

Now and then
I work upon a remnant of ivory silk;
Shot with tincture of Vermillion and soft violet,
stitching beads of crystal garland in pastiche
For my pleasure gown.

Bordered
With tissue of gold, and silver foil.
Portable software and glittering microcosm
Of processed words and music:
A parachute for the hard earth.

And here
Among the fragrance of many roses,
It is my pleasure to lightly sew,
The precious threads of art together
And take my quiet ease.

Before
I am drawn again to the Sharp edge
Of the precipice; and plunged into the clamorous sea
Of vagrant life; I will make a place to be happy in.

Gill Bazovsky
1984

MEMORIES OF BLUEBELLS IN THE CHURNET VALLEY
(below Alton Towers)

By quiet hedgerows,
Along a furrowed lane I made my way.
When, from a distant corner,
A wreath of blue smoke curled.
At the bend I came upon them, in the grass.
The old hedger and the boy without a care,
Watching the flames, they came from yesterday.
Greeting me friendly as I passed.
Later, returning, I saw the boy
Gathering bluebells in his broad arms.
'For his grandmother the hedger said,
'I mind when I was young, a carpet
blue on the far side of the track,
we saw them from the train.
Go and find them if you can'. He said
and his eyes were filled with bluebells.
Now backwards I drift to yesterday,
Along the horizon of a high green meadow,
Where shadows of enchanted trees flicker,
Between the fingers of the setting sun,
and old woods plunge down steep hillsides,
in the timeless valley;

I came upon the bluebells Endymion,
they shimmered softly as a haze of mist
Touched the deep green of their criss-crossed leaves,
Shaded by ancient firs on the fringe of a dark wood,
where silver birch trees whispered in the bracken;
I laid me down near the blue carpet and became one with the earth.

Gill Bazovsky

Margaret Bevan

POETIC INJUSTICE

I wish I could pinpoint the time when it started but it's impossible. If I could, perhaps I could have stopped it, this infernal, tortuous jealousy that rises up through my body like an all-consuming virus. I have tried to stem the tide but it refuses to abate. So, I have to assume it is not really my fault, its unstoppable and I am a slave to it, a guy that has to accept that it is part of his DNA. It became more evident during my creative writing degree course, although I tried desperately to hide it. Everyone else seemed so much more gifted than me, seemed to be able to write without fear and not worry about reading out their efforts. It didn't help that I looked like a geek, tall, lanky with horned rimmed glasses and never ever able to grow a beard, that's me. Of course, there were those who, like me, were scared witless to open their mouths and naturally I gravitated towards them becoming something bordering on friends. However, in the second year everything changed. I started to really enjoy the poetry modules, finding solace in the words of others and somehow finding my own sombre style. I was surprised and elated when Mr Harrison chose a couple of my poems to be featured in an upcoming literary evening. The great and the good of the faculty were there and my efforts were amply rewarded with many lovely comments and much praise. My star was in the ascendant, I had made it, or so I thought. This was my calling and I focussed on compiling a book of poetry that I was sure would make my fortune.

Fast forward 10 years and here I am, leaning against my delivery bike whilst standing outside a coffee shop. I'm drinking a take-away cappuccino, staring across the road at the Leonardo Royal Hotel. That all consuming virus is welling up again as I think of her inside that building being lauded as a short-listed author in the Jackie Collins Award for Romantic Thrillers. How crass is that, hardly the Booker is it, but more galling is that it will probably mean she will sell even more of the drivel that passes for fiction these days.

Ester, one of the other Deliveroo bike riders, is the one to blame for this turn of events. She mentioned last year that she had made a delivery to one of her favourite authors, Olivia Hurst, and wanted everyone to see the selfie she had taken with her. I did a double take. Olivia may be her pseudonym but I remember her as Jane Wells. Ester proceeded to tell me that Olivia was minted with a house in Shoreditch worth a fortune. I could picture her in uni with chestnut brown braided hair and long flowing skirts with no great stand out moments where the written word was concerned. The virus infiltrated me then and it has slowly gripped me day by day, I am possessed.

My beanie hat and denim jacket aren't doing anything to keep out the cold tonight and I'm just about to leave when I spot her coming down the hotel steps. Well, money can certainly make you look a million dollars that's for sure. No hint of the cheap boho fashion from student days, beautifully cut designer clothes for our Jane these days. That feeling is rising again and this time I am completely enveloped by it. She hails a taxi; I know she doesn't live far away and jump on my bike and follow. Nothing suspicious in a delivery driver going like the wind on the London streets and I have become very very fit doing this mind numbingly boring job. As my speed increases so does my anger and my need to right this injustice. When I did my research, I realised that Jane had started out writing nonsense for Mills and Boon. God how desperate do you have to be for recognition to sell your literary soul to that particular devil. We are nearing her home turf now and I am consumed by this rage that is getting stronger and stronger. Those endless rejection letters from publishers looking down their nose at me are etched into my brain. The endless menial jobs I took on just to be able to self-publish my work and for what? A few measly pounds here and there while she gets to earn a fortune by doling out claptrap. The cab pulls up and she climbs out, here's my chance. I park up and cross the road and start to follow her up the path. There is a full moon and I can see her clearly put the key in the lock and I am about to lunge forward as I hear her shout.

'Only me Mum, you OK, where's Sam?'
I see a frail elderly lady in the hallway. She's sitting crumpled in a wheelchair and I hear her scream out.

'Go away, who are you, you don't live here, get out, get out.' She sounds terrified.

The front door closes and now I can only her muffled shouting.

I'm dumbfounded, what the hell was that? I walk back down the path and cross over the road to my bike. I stand there for what seems like an age.

The front door opens again and out dashes a male nurse or a carer not sure which. He's heading in my direction and talking very fast on his phone.
'Yes I'm on my way now, I promise I'll be home asap. Ok, ok, I know but I couldn't leave, tough shift and Lydia was late. Oh c'mon, she hardly ever goes out these days and she's paying me extra so it's all good and guess what, she won, yes, she won.'

He was in his car and gone and I'm still standing here staring at the house. The vicious virus in my brain has vanished, the rage has subsided and all that's left is deflation and utter and absolute shame.

Margaret Bevan
June 2023

DERAILED

The wet stone walls of the disused railway tunnel glistened like polished coal. The musty smell of stagnant urine invaded her nostrils. His unmistakeable raucous laugh echoed through the cavernous vault whilst flames leapt from their make-shift brazier. He spotted her as the others swigged their poison of choice. Why choose this hellhole over home with her? His eyes said go, leave me alone, too late, she was at his side pulling, begging him, she won. As they left, he removed his filthy scarf revealing his white dog collar.
 "All they need is someone who'll listen"
"So do I dad"

Margaret Bevan
100 word Flash Fiction
June 2023

JUST THE JOB

'Hiya, can you hear me, sorry, shocking signal here. Well, I got the job, well, not THE job, not the one I thought I was going for.

Oh, you know me, well of course you do, but what I mean is, you know me of old. I've never been what you'd call a details person, have I? More big picture that's me. Yes, yes I know you've told me often enough read the small print Kathy, blah blah blah. So, okay on this occasion perhaps you would have been right, but, that ad definitely said 'Au pair' I think. Listen Sis, what it definitely didn't say was General Dog's Body. I mean Sue would I have applied for it if it had? Hell, no I would not. Well, maybe in my current strained circumstances, port, storm etc., but in the general scheme of things the barge pole would definitely not have even scraped, leave alone touched.

Got to say amazing house, pillars, massive driveway, wrought iron balconies, dread to think how many millions it cost. Now, should I have twigged as soon as she, that's Mrs prissy knickers, the lady of the house, opened the shiny red door? Probably, I tell you girl, she stood there in her designer jump suit and Bond Street jewellery and scanned me from head to foot with that look, you know THE look. It sort of said 'I'm Hampstead, you're Hackney'. I nearly said, "You're no better than me Mrs", but I kept that up my sleeve for later. Well, anyway, she takes me into the kitchen, oh lovely it was, all gleaming white and chrome with black granite tops, you know the kinda thing. Mind you, I don't think a roast dinner with three veg is her thing. Nah, I reckon all their grub gets delivered from Harrods and goes ping, if you gets my drift. Oh, I was licking my lips when I saw them cupcakes on the cake stand though. Luckily, I didn't touch, close up I realized they was all bone china! Hilarious.

She says the kids are in boarding school for most of the year so I'll only see them when they gets holidays. Imagine, 9 and 7 they are mind, sent away to heaven knows where. Strangers barking orders at them all day long when they probably thought they were going to be flying around on broomsticks and having Harry Potter adventures, poor little mites. You and me well, we might not have had much but we did ave love didn't we? Well, when the old man wasn't giving us a clip for being cheeky, well, me mostly.

So, then her ladyship gives me a list of all my so-called duties. I tell you it was as long as a bog roll. Recycling rubbish, sweeping the paths round the garden, loading and unloading washing machine and dishwasher etcetera etcetera as well as all the hoovering, dusting and washing floors. Then she says she will give me a day's trial if you please. Cheek of it, I nearly told her where to stick her job but I thought, no, keep it up your sleeve for later. Then she goes off in her posh car to meet friends for lunch. Oh, you should have seen her motor, it weren't no Ford Focus I can tell you. I dunno the make but it was champagne colour with a soft top, absolutely stunning.

So, I thought to myself 'Right then girl, let's show Mrs Bouquet shall we. I'll do a Lewis Hamilton, get as much done on that poxy list of hers as quick as lightning and she'll be begging me to stay.' Of course, if I hadn't been going quite so fast, I wouldn't have smashed that Doulton vase. Stupid if you ask me putting something valuable like that on a hall table where it can be accidentally bumped by a Vax, asking for trouble that is. Also, cos I was rushing, I didn't see that tiny weeny patch of water on the ceramic floor tiles in the kitchen that made me go arse over tip when I was taking all those food waste bags out. But it definitely wasn't my fault that the blasted Cockapoo ripped them all open before I could pick them up. Oh my God, there was bits of rotting food everywhere. I had a right old tussle getting that chow mein out of his jaws. Then he was sick cos he scoffed some over-ripe avocados. That took ages to clean up. Also, you got any ideas how to get the smell of kippers out of a shag pile carpet – it's a cream one an all to make matters worse.

But you know me, I just kept on going regardless, working my way through that never ending list of hers. Now, I was doing really well till the sweeping brush came off its handle. Trouble was I was going at such a lick round them paths that it literally flew, somersaulted in the air and went straight through a glass pane in the green house setting off some sort of sprinkler system. Now that definitely wasn't my fault. But, and here's where Sis you get to say I told you so, I do own up to the fact that I didn't thoroughly read all the instructions for what she wanted me to do regarding the pond. Well, now there's a heron circling above, all the koi carp fish are lying dead and so I reckon am I when Hyacinth gets back. Now, I'm gonna text you the address, and please, please get round here and pick me up sharpish. You can't miss the house it's the one with the fire brigade outside, I'll explain all when you get here. Love you, bye bye, bye.'

Margaret Bevan
June 2023

ARRIVEDERCI RHONDDA

Marco's Italian café has been the hub of Pontycwm for nearly 60 years. It has played host to amateur psychologists, philosophers, would be politicians and social activists over the years, all putting the world to rights. Young couples have flirted here over a frothy coffee until dusk became night with music wafting from the jukebox whilst providing a romantic backdrop to their first flush of love. No doubt the cost of its modern-day counterpart cappuccino or latte would have rendered those dreamy lovers speechless and definitely penniless. Many original features still remain, the first ever mock marble soda fountain brought over from the old country and the etched mirrored wall still glistening behind glass shelves supporting fluted ice-cream dishes. The warm coffee bean and cocoa powder aroma, which have pervaded the walls for decades, has cheered many a rain sodden customer. Twin brothers Paulo and Lorenzo run the business now since their father Marco retired but the old man can't resist popping in daily to keep an eye on things.

"Morning Dai, you're late this morning," Paulo greeted one of their regulars with his customary beaming smile.

"Aye, Mille's not well, she's had a bad throat all weekend, trouble is it's not completely closed up yet so I can still hear her nagging me." Dai gives a rye chuckle as he mounts the four steps to the seating area at the rear of the café.

"Oh, don't say that," Will winced at his friend's throwaway comment,
"what I'd give to hear Joan nagging me today." Dai lowered his eyes as he reached their table.

"Where's Don then? I thought he'd have been here bright and early today." Dai was eager to change the subject as he was uncomfortable with sentiment.

"Well, he said 'see you a fortnight Monday' when I saw him up the Labour Club before he went off to Blackpool," said Will.
Don had visited his sister in Blackpool for two weeks in April every year since she moved away.

Dai Price, Will Jenkins and Don Thomas had met at Marco's every morning, except Sundays, for over 20 years. They'd all been born in 1936, and aged 15 had descended in the steel cage to the abyss of the coalface. The 1980's saw them all lose their jobs along with thousands of others when Ian McGregor's hearse stealthily collected the battered coffin that had once been the proud mining industry in this and all the surrounding valleys.

The 10 o'clock meetings at Marco's had started after Don's wife died of cancer, the year they were all made redundant. No job, no wife, no real reason to live, Don had not coped well. Dai and Will feared for his sanity and decided to meet every morning to give his day some purpose. When Will, the gentle giant of the trio, lost his wife to heart disease nearly 5 years ago, the morning gatherings became even more important. The Ponty Three had become just as much of an institution as the café itself, sitting at the same table every day with a standing order of regular coffee and toast for three.

Behind the café's pristine white marble counter, Paulo and Lorenzo were busy serving customers. Paulo, the good looking one and the salesman of the duo, was always flirting with the ladies and managing to get them to divulge the latest village gossip. He was tall; broad shouldered blessed with thick wavy hair, which along with his moustache was greying rapidly now. Lorenzo had gone bald quite young and was taller and slimmer than his twin. He was considered to be much more serious and didn't engage in as much idle banter. However, this morning they were whispering excitedly to each other whenever the counter was empty.

"Well, do you think he will come in today," Lorenzo shot a furtive glance to the left and up to the table where the three friends always sat.

"God knows," Paolo giggled, "which is probably right you know, he probably does know after yesterday. You could have knocked me down with a feather when Don walked into our church with his lady friend." He let out a slow, almost inaudible whistle.
"What are Tweedledum and Tweedledee going to make of her I wonder," Lorenzo raised his dark bushy eyebrows at his brother.

They didn't have too long to wait for an answer. The café windows gave a panoramic view of the narrow main street and Lorenzo spotted the couple crossing the road from the butcher's shop opposite. He nudged his brother and they both pretended to busy themselves, vigorously cleaning imaginary stains on the counter. Don opened the café door engaging the loud bell as he motioned for his lady companion to enter first. His green eyes were sparkling and he smoothed his short silver hair flat as he closed the door.

"Morning Don," Paulo greeted him with a smile, "glad to see you're back, the other musketeers have been lost without you," he gestured up to the other two.
"Oh, I'm sure they've coped. Usual for me please and Ebele likes her coffee strong and black please."

Don mounted the stairs as his friends stared incredulously.
"Alright boys, how's it going, let me introduce you to Ebele." He turned to his new friend and said in a sweeter tone, "Ebele these are my good friends Dai and Will that I've been telling you

about. Well, say hello boys, cat got your tongue."

His comrades spluttered some quick hellos as Don and Ebele took their seats.
Don hastily recounted his trip to Blackpool, telling his friends that he had met Ebele at a tea dance and they had hit it off straight away. He had invited her to Pontycwm for a few days so that she could see where he lived. From then on the conversation became stilted with Don desperately trying to get his friends to include Ebele in the conversation but the atmosphere was strained.

Lorenzo brought the order to the table and shook hands with Ebele.

   "Nice to meet you again, hope everyone made you welcome last night." He glanced quickly to gauge a reaction from the others.

   "Oh, everyone was so friendly," Ebele put a stress on the last word, "your Church is so like mine in Blackpool but of course very different from my church in Ghana." Ebele smiled broadly at Lorenzo and her brilliant white teeth contrasted vibrantly with her smooth ebony skin, so smooth it was quite impossible to guess her age.

"Buongiorno Papa," Paulo greeted Marco as the old man came through the cafe door and they chatted away in Italian at machine-gun speed for several minutes whilst Marco dispensed his father's morning double espresso.

At eighty-one Marco was still ramrod erect, priding himself on his fitness. He climbed nimbly up the four steps to the seating area, greeted the table of four and sat on the table opposite.

"Hi Marco," wheezed Will. Emphysema had been his inheritance following his many years under ground.

Over the next thirty minutes Marco watched as the woman was virtually ignored by Dai and Will and witnessed Don trying desperately to include her at every opportunity but finally giving up.

"Well, we have to love you and leave you now boys, Ebele wants to make an appointment at the hairdressers," Don's tone was brusque and his awkwardness blatantly obvious.

"It's been so nice to meet you both, Don never stops talking about the two of you so it was lovely to put faces to the names." Ebele shook hands with both of them, stared them both in the eye and flashed a warm smile, bravely masking her true feelings.

After the couple left the café Will and Dai were left to discuss the situation.
"I'm gob smacked, what the hell is he doing with that woman," said Dai quietly." He was clearly oblivious to Marco eavesdropping.
"He's really excelled himself hasn't he. I know one thing; he's going to be hard pressed to find a pint of Welsh bitter in Ghana" Will added. Both men started to laugh.
Marco could contain himself no longer. He rose and came and sat at their table.
"Well boys, I think it's you that have excelled yourselves," his coal black eyes glared at the two of them and they knew he meant business.

"Oh, we're only having a laugh Marco, we didn't mean anything by it," Dai's voice quavered slightly as, in his younger days, the café owner's temper had been legendary.

"No, you were making insulting remarks about that lady, that's no laughing matter. I thought Don was your friend?" He watched them shuffle uncomfortably in their seats and was determined that they would squirm and wriggle some more.

"No, no it's just that she was, well, different. We were taken aback a bit, that's all." Dai was on the defensive

"Really. Funny isn't it how times change. Here we are, 2006 and my friend Emilio in Cardiff well his son Luigi, opened an Italian restaurant in the Bay last year and people are flocking there and spending over sixty pound a night." Dai and Will glanced at each other not knowing where the old timer was going with this one.

"'Cos of course, I can still remember wartime and being called a 'bloody eye-tie' and worse as a mob stoned the ice-cream cart." The listeners looked on in disbelief. Marco continued

"You know, I've finally come to grips with the Internet. I've learned many wonderful things from it. I even found information on there about how they are trying to get the government to say sorry for my papa Gino's death."

Gino Rossi, Marco's father, had come to the Rhondda in 1902 when he was only eight years old. He worked in his uncle's café until 1919 when he married Isabella and opened his own café.

"You boys are too young to remember the start of the last war, but my family soon found out what prejudice was like. I was only nineteen when Churchill said,
'Collar the lot.' I was sent to camps all over Britain just for being Italian. I ended up on the Isle of Man. I didn't get back home until 1946." The old man's dark eyes were filling with tears.

"When I returned here my family had been destroyed. My father Gino had been sent to Canada on the "Arandora Star." That ship was torpedoed and he was one of four hundred and eighty-six Italians who lost their lives." His voice was steadily rising in pitch

"Italians like him had been working here for decades, we came from the poorest parts of Italy just to find work." He thumped the table and the two men jumped.
"We worked seven days a week, members of this community, but it didn't make a blind bit of difference. The government branded us all as fascists and sent us to the four corners of the world." The old man removed his spectacles and wiped his eyes with a freshly laundered handkerchief as the pair looked on uneasily.

"Mama died of a broken heart they said and then my sister ended up in a mental home because she thought she had lost everyone. All that was left was this, just bricks and mortar." He leaned across the table and opened his eyes as wide as possible

"Just remember, when you needed a refuge from heartbreak and humdrum lives you found it here in my place. My papa and me, we found no such sanctuary back then because we were 'different'. What I want to know is when did I stop being this terribly dangerous alien: stop being 'different' and suddenly become everyone's best friend again."

Marco rose from his seat, descended the four steps with head erect, leaving Dai and Will stunned and staring into their empty cups.

Margaret Bevan
August 2023

Judith Blakemore

'Jasmine Floral Arch'
Watercolour.

'Tiffany Lamp at 11 O'clock'
Pen and Ink and Watercolour.

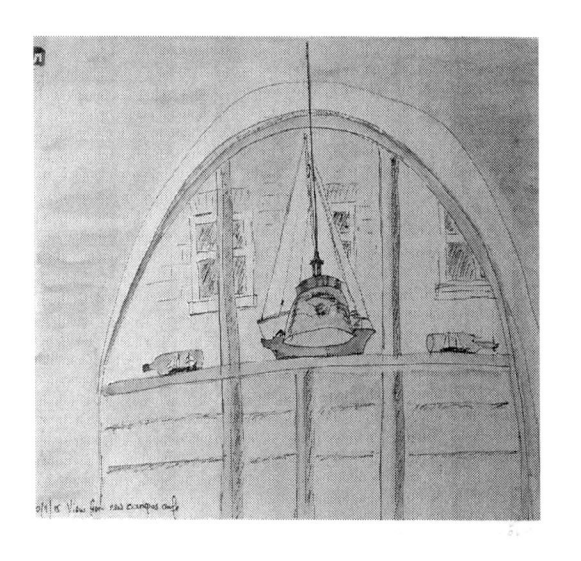

'Ship on a ledge'
Pen and Ink and Watercolour.

'Steve Ferris in composition'
Acrylic on canvas.

Ken Blakemore

LOVE DUET

This door is alarmed:
the woman at the till is falling
Caution! Please check before alighting
in love with a customer
as the platform may not be as long as the train
and she's already opening the door.

Staff notice: please question all strangers
who enter the shop this morning.
Fortunes can go down as well as up; the Earth
swaying beneath her feet as he glances past,
colliding with Mercury a billion years from now,
his star apparently not congruent with hers.

But wait, the pound has risen against the euro
and she shivers – her fingers
at market close ending up on the day
in his, after all. He'd purchased a cappuccino,
please think before you throw this cup away
an excuse to stay
magnetised; pulled back by her gravity.

Later, at sunset,
a neon sign's letters say
We Let Houses...
'Do what?' they laughed,
together.

Ken Blakemore
December 2013

THE ACCOMPANIER

I expected a grim figure waiting:
A dark cloak; sallow male face;
The rasp of the rusty boat side
Scraping the gritting bank.

But no, we came to a little hut;
Small, in the woods,
A friendly stovepipe poking up;
Aromatic wood smoke curling -
Ash or oak, I think.

We knock the skewed door and wait;
Inside, yellow lantern light
Shines through the cracks.
Voices still.

Through open door we see three, no four,
On a bench drinking tea.
"Are you sure?" asks the woman,
Putting down her mug.
She's smiling, a little reluctant;
"Are you sure?" she says again,
Reaching for her coat.

She smells of earth, and pine, and berries;
Her hand is warm and dry.
She flings a cloak around me
As I say goodbye.

And now it's time for her to lead me
Under trees, along a path,
Past the fox, the owl, the cat,
Towards the fence and kiss-gate
Which, opening wide, by itself,
Creaks a smile.

Ken Blakemore
03.06.2017

Joey Clarke

BLUEFIELDS

My father lays in a field of daisies; unbeknown to him a giant earwig is making its way across his face, final destination, my Dad's left ear. He brushes the irritant away, oblivious to its identity. I am about three years old as I clamour onto his torso, seeking some approval and recognition. He is oblivious to me too, just like the earwig, as I stare at his closed eyes, lost in a world of wild women, wine and the piano tune. I stare at the black hairs protruding from his nose, this is the closest I've got to my father for as long as I can remember. He is unaware of my presence. I catch sight of our sheepdog, Spot, who also clamours for my father's attention, waking him up in the process. He gives a heart wrenching shriek, brushing the infallible insect again off his face "Aah, it's an earwig – an earwig!" leaping up and dashing into the house in frenzy. Spot and myself are left in an entangled heap in the surrounding flowers as I stare at the brilliantly blue sky; I feel lost in this perfumed paradise, and wishing to be enveloped in its magnificence. It's strange how it's the little things that we recall from childhood.

Growing up on an eleven acre smallholding, I often wondered why the place was called Bluefields, and realised, when much older, it was because of the orchard carpeted bluebells, which gave off the most intoxicating fragrance. We lay there fore a while, amongst the butterflies, yellow ochre, ultramarine blue and earth orange, their flapping wings having a hypnotic effect, as we both doze in the heat of early summer. Two tunes spring to mind when I remember my childhood; the hypnotic sound of the cuckoo in early Summer, and the nursery rhyme 'Jack and Jill' the lyrics of which I insisted on singing as a child, whilst accompanying my Grandmother to fetch our own pail of water. Holding my grandmother's hand tightly, I skipped across the fields gleefully singing this tune.

Suddenly, a piercing scream cuts through the air like a lightening bolt, shattering my idyll. 'Why did she have to spoil everything?' My mother's wailing could be heard from the farmhouse, competing with the cawing of the crows, an interruption to my perfect paradise. As I catch my grandmother's eyes, she says something about returning for the picnic, having already packed the basket of delicious treats; welsh cakes, jam tarts, a variety of freshly cut sandwiches. The piercing words "...and Mammy is coming too" evaporated my excitement and later the three of us trudged towards our picnic destination, dodging the sheep droppings and carcasses, and my mother walking sheepishly behind. The sweet smell of the honeysuckle and foxglove penetrates the otherwise heavily sour air.

Like a pathway of shadows, I recall my mother, Jean, from a distance. Her ever changing personality, making me dance around her, eager to please, never quite touching. To do so, would have been hard to bear, like searing my seven year old feet on hot coals. And she could be kind, excruciatingly so; opening her childlike purse with its few pitiful pennies. "Go on, have them," she would plead, desperate for my love and attention, as I'd recoil holding and hiding under my grandmother's pleated skirts. Finding ingenious places in which to hide from my mother's wrath, because a favourite pastime, both real and imaginative. Sheltering under the umbrella of the gnarled oak in the orchard, my childhood pain, sharp as pins, running through its hollowed branches, an infusion of colour and teeming with wildlife; this was my safe haven as a child, in which to hide from the frequent dramas of the household. Echoes of my mother could still be heard, but mostly drowned by the sweet smell of sweet Williams, mint and the orchestral melodies of the birds nesting. Ti was a terrific hiding place as a child, there, amongst the towering fruit trees, their branches, steps to the sunlight, of which I frequently climbed. And, as I lay amongst the carpet of fallen fruit, memories of my childhood begin to surface, flooding my mind.

Pound, pound, my mother's steps could be heard, firstly on the landing, and then on each step of the stairway, as I started to shake and look for ways to escape. A favourite place was the attic, but I would have to pass her on the stairway to reach this destination, which was out of the question. I would make my escape as soon as she entered the living room, dashing past her like a silent breeze, she would not even notice. And once there, I had entered my favourite imaginary world, where no one dared to enter, without my per=mission. In the attic, I was Queen of the Castle, and not the powerless, invisible waif I felt in the real world where my tormented mother ruled the roost. My castle was filled with all sorts of toys, most of which were disregarded by the parents of other children on the common land surrounding our small holding. These toys were all faulty in some way, a one arm Sindy doll, a broken etch-a-sketch, and a battered orange space hopper that had seen better days, with its original gleeful owner, a tiny tears doll, discarded, minus her clothes, and an assortment of colourful toys and books 'Rupert the Bear' and 'The Little Match Girl' being my favourites; all squeezed into cardboard boxes of various shapes and sizes. I would spend hours by myself up there, oblivious to the commotion and drama enfolding downstairs. Lost in a world of fantasy and adventure, the colourful images and exciting tales in the books carrying me away into distant lands, which I would never want to return from.

I don't remember much about my mother, Jean, until she arrived from Woodlands, the local sanitarium, suitcase in hand; I must have been about seven years old, with an almighty chip on my shoulder as this virtual stranger embedded herself within the family, with a sense of entitlement, become a tyrant in the process.

Jean was late for work that morning. Highly nervous by nature, she dreaded the thought of her boss finding out, so she gingerly stepped past his office hoping not to be seen. The family bakers where she worked was run by father and son and employed many locals in the village. "You're OK, they haven't arrived yet." Shouted one of her workmates and Jean, reassured, breathed a sigh of relief. Although she enjoyed working at the bakers, she was wary of the Boss's son Luke, in particular. He would stare at Jean for what seemed like hours, undressing her with his eyes, and, because he was management, she felt an 'upstairs, downstairs' beholding to him. Jean would return his smile, trying not to give him any encouragement. Anyway, she was not interested in Luke, having met someone recently and saw a future with him.

After lunch with her workmates, which consisted of the usual banter, laughter and juicy gossip, she decided to clean the walk in cupboard. It had been a long hot day working in the bakery, however, she relished the company of her workmates, which made the otherwise intense atmosphere with the roar of the oven machinery, tolerable. Jean carefully placed all the bags of plain and self-raising flour neatly in a row on the appropriate shelves, followed by tins of syrup, jars of different flavoured jams, together with yeast and baking powder; the bakery, having received a major delivery that morning, all the groceries had to be stacked neatly on the shelves. Jean breathed a sigh of relief. At least she could work in peace, away from the intimidating gaze of Luke. She began singing softly to herself, daydreaming of meeting her new fella that evening. They had planned a cinema date and then some supper at a local restaurant in the village; she hoped this relationship would last. She was to be her sister Margaret's bridesmaid at her forthcoming wedding, and wanted to be married herself very soon. Lost in thought, she placed another tin of syrup on the shelf and suddenly she felt the grip of strong arms holding her around the waist. She recognised Luke's husky voice whispering in her ear. "This is your life." he cackled, as she detected the faint smell of alcohol on his breath, tinged with perspiration. She started to feel dizzy and lose consciousness.

"Jean, Jean, wake up. Please wake up." The combination of her mother's voice and her face being slapped, made her jolt awake. Although she recognised her mother's voice earlier, she did not recognise the concerned faces of the strangers surround her and felt very scared, in what was the familiar surrounding of Bluefields, her family home. Jean started to scream, running around the farmhouse in an effort to escape. She did not know what was happening to her.

"Jean, Jeanie, wake up." She opened her eyes slowly and looked around. She noticed the white clinical walls, with a few floral paintings for decoration. She tried to move her arms but they were strapped tightly and firmly to the bed. Again, concerned faces watched her intently. This time a male and female, dressed in all white starched uniforms; she must be in some type of hospital, she thought. "You are in Ward E, Woodlands Hospital." The female nurse's clipped professional tone, jolted Jean wide awake. She was just seventeen years old and so desperately wanted to return to her parents at 'Bluefields'.

"Where is she?" thought Evan. They were due to meet at 7.30 p.m. outside this cinema. "Hadn't she said she really wanted to watch this particular film, hadn't she?" Evan again glanced nervously at his watch. Looking around, there was no sign of Jean and the film was about to start. "Where could she be?" A feeling of profound disappointment started to dominate his being; meeting Jean at the local dance a week ago, her vibrance had brought an infusion of colour to his rather dull and monotonous life. Her smile setting his senses on fire and filling his lonely heart with an orchestral melody.

Joey Clarke

Steve Cound

A TALE OF THE PENLLERGAER WOODS

The Lovers Ring

Roger was texting again;

"Hi Chris, Sandy and I were just remarking what a damp, boring and flat day today is after all the joy and liveliness of yesterday. Oh well!"

Chris to Roger:

"Go for a walk. It lifts the spirits 😄"

Roger to Chris:

"Glad I took your advice Chris. I went up to Penllergaer Wood and found a film crew!!!! On the end of the Lower Lake, nearest to Fforestfach. It will probably be shown on Amazon and it's title is "Excalibur Rising". Lots of burly blokes in plastic chain mail and some of them with 'tomato Ketchup' on their faces and a one armed dummy in the make up tent surrounded by girls doing I don't know what to him."

Chris to Roger:

"Ha! Sounds like a laugh. I'll have to keep my eyes open for the film."

Roger to Chris:

"And so Christine, whilst I was sat there on the bench by the stream texting you, I noticed what I took to be a piece of golden wrapping paper that somebody had carelessly dropped half buried in the mud. I dug it out to bin it and to my astonishment it turned out to be a ring; Golden, ladies sized, with a hallmark, which I can't read 'cause it's full of mud."

I felt like Bilbo Baggins for a moment there Chris............................

............and so I slipped the ring onto my little finger and all of a sudden my head started spinning and I slumped back down onto the bench to avoid slipping into the stream and I discovered that I was now wearing a deer-stalker, a rubber Macintosh, tweed trousers and gaiters and I had gained a gun-dog to go along with the shotgun at my side and most significantly for my tale, I had arrived in the middle of an argument between two lovers on the other side of the stream.

Anyone could see that it was a love that could never be; he was in workman' clothes, mud stained boots and trousers, his screwed up cloth cap clutched nervously in his calloused hands, whilst his screwed up face protested his love and devotion for his well dressed lover from 'The Big House'.

All through these long summer evenings, he James had been foreman in charge of the powder crew, blasting their way through the rock to form the long carriageway that would take the master, John Dillwyn Llewelyn, and his lady in their Hansom Cab down to meet their fine London friends in Fforestfach and bring them back to Penllergaer House to indulge their passion for all matters scientific and even for this new fangled hobby of photography. But all of that was over now; the blasting was finished, he had had a handsome bonus for early completion and was now ready to move on. He had caught the eye of Isambard Kingdom Brunel who was proposing a revolutionary new "suspended" bridge across the Avon gorge and he wanted James to help him with some particularly tricky foundations.

But the fat bankroll in his pocket meant nothing to this lovely creature standing opposite him, and as he reached out to touch the auburn curls at the nape of that lovely neck, which itself was framed by that soft lace collar, he heard a soft sigh come from those pouting lips. It sounded like the last soft breeze of summer, but it could have been the harbinger of the winter storms for he knew his lover had an icy temper. Both their mothers and their fathers would have been mortified to know that this illicit love had been going on all summer long.

In desperation James had bought a gold ring from the Dolaucothi gold mine up in Carmarthenshire but as he reverently brought it from his breeches pocket his lover reached out and softly closed James's fingers around it. "No James," his sweetheart said, "this can never be, Mama is getting frightfully suspicious, and they would cut me orf without a penny if this ever leaked out. I know our fortunes have sunk pretty low with Papa's waterways investments paying such rotten dividends now that the railways are coming, but we still have our good name and our standing in the community, this would kill them both. Can't we both look back on this as a fine summer romance that withered and perished with chills of autumn, and anyway we are returning to St John's Wood on Monday and you are going to Bristol."

James knew the truth when he heard it, and he was mature enough to accept it, so with a last lingering kiss they parted company for ever. James to his world of heavy engineering, innovation and excitement and his beau back to the world of soiree's, afternoon teas, fine clothes and keeping up appearances.

But as James walked away, only I saw him deliberately drop the ring on the bank of the River Lan and grind it under his heel where I would find it nearly 200 years later and only I could see that James, after his success in Clifton and other places would end his days as a respected parliamentarian in Queen Victoria's government.

And as for his lover, well his lover died in the heat of battle in Afghanistan, 1842, near the Khyber Pass, cut down by a crazed Pashtun warrior. He was buried with full military honours as Major Sir Christopher Passmore DSO and he was quite right, it never would have worked, for you see the' love that dare not speak its name' between two men was still a hanging offence and had been since the days of the Merry Monarch, Henry V111.

Steve Cound

DEATH RAY MATTHEWS

On Wednesday last, on a sunny afternoon, I drove up past Morriston Hospital and took the Rhydypandy Road known as "the back road to Ammanford", up over Mynydd y Gwair, where the sky is big and I mean huge; where osprey, red kite and skylark take the place of pigeon, magpie and blackbird.

I was looking for the last mortal home of Harry Grindall Matthews, inventor of the first remote controlled vehicle, and the infamous "Death Ray", writer of celestial messages on the clouds, inventor of the first mobile phone, of the first talking film the list just goes on. I finally found the bungalow that he built, by way of various serendipitous coincidences at a point where you can see not only the Gower Peninsular and Burry Holm but also by just shifting your gaze Swansea Bay and clear across to Port Talbot.

I decided not to risk my suspension on the rough track, so I left the Seat and trudged past the sign that read "The Ranch", up and around the bend. The bungalow was securely barb-wired in just as it was in Harry's time, but the barking of half a dozen dogs alerted the owner, who when he noticed me shouted "Two minutes". Whilst I waited for him to shut the dogs up I watched his Welsh Cobs, one of which was giving a young sapling a really hard time by obsessively scratching his backside on it and the other two could obviously feel the sap rising by their play fighting and rearing up on each other.

The smallholder turned out to be a remarkably sociably fellow with all the time in the world to talk about his illustrious and even infamous predecessor.
Harry Grindall Matthews was born 17th March 1880 in Winterbourne, Gloucester he studied at the Merchant Venturers School in Bristol and continued his education in the fledgeling field of electronic engineering, he fought in the Boer War and as a member of Baden-Powell's South African Constabulary, he was twice wounded and subsequently decorated. After the war he worked for a consulting engineer at Bexhill who allowed him to develop his ideas for wireless-telephony which he dubbed the Aerophone, then in 1911 he sent a radio message to the

noted early pilot C.B. Hucks who was flying at 700 feet, whilst he himself was on Ely racecourse, Cardiff, the first ever such radio communication, and only eight years after the Wright Bros pioneering flight. Harry also sent the first Press message from Newport to Cardiff. The following year he was "Commanded" to demonstrate his invention before King George V, where at Buckingham Palace he established communication between two cars in motion. The government were interested but Mathews insisted that no experts be present at any demonstration and when four observers started dismantling his apparatus he drove them away and cancelled the event. At first the War Office claimed the demonstration was a failure but then the press rushed to his defence as they strangely, continued to do throughout his career and the government backed down and said that it was all a misunderstanding.

In 1914 the British Government announced a prize of £25,000 to the inventor who could remotely control unmanned vehicles. Matthews demonstrated a model boat to The Admiralty using Selenium celled batteries on Richmond

Park's Penn Pond and received the prize money but strangely his system was never used. By 1921 Harry had turned his attention to recording soundtracks onto film, and made a talking movie of an interview with Sir Ernest Shackleton prior to his final departure for the Antarctic and this was six years before Warner Bros brought out The Jazz Singer. But as Al Jolson remarked "You Ain't Heard Nothing Yet!" by 1924 newspapers were carrying headlines of "Death Ray" Mathews. Harry was experimenting with electrically charged light beams which he claimed could stop an aeroplane engine by putting its magnetos out of action, it would explode gunpowder or kill a mouse at a distance. During experiments it was not unusual for a passing technician to be knocked out or burned if he got in the way. Harry himself claimed to have lost the use of an eye during these experiments, and if you look at an absolutely marvellous Pathe Newsreel film that Harry created it is not hard to see why. Some of the images look to be straight out of Hollywood and that is where he was headed next but with a typically dramatic exit.

On May 27th, 1924 the High Court granted an injunction to stop him selling the rights to his Death Ray abroad, but when Major Wimperis arrived at Harry's laboratory to negotiate a new deal he had already left. His investors also turned up and rushed to Croydon airport to stop him leaving the country, but his plane was just taking off, his departure strangely recorded on film.

Whilst in America, Harry Mathews worked for Warner Bros developing his ideas of sound recordings on film and the 1936 Flash Gordon cinema serial starring Buster Crabbe featured a lot of props or "Special Effects" as we would call them today that are very familiar from the Pathé News film.

In 1925 Harry invented what he called the "Luminaphone", an organ that was played by means of light beams; Harry said "My tone wheel can reproduce any and every musical work with the skill of an orchestra and the tonal quality of a grand organ;" also whilst in Hollywood he developed his "Sky Projector" for casting images onto the clouds. In fact at

Christmas time in 1930, the people of Hampstead, London were amazed to see the image of a "Voluptuous" angel with outstretched wings flying across the sky, followed by the words "A Happy Christmas", and a clock telling the real time. He demonstrated it again in New York but this invention like a lot of his others was not commercially successful.

In fact by 1931 Harry was facing bankruptcy; It seems to me that he was brilliant at what he was doing, in a completely new field with few competitors, like an early Bill Gates or Steve Jobs. But he had no head for business and perhaps because of past bad experiences could find no one that he could trust to deal for him. Of course it didn't help that he spent most of his investors money in expensive hotels!

Anyway by 1934, Harry had a new set of investors and had relocated to Mynnydd y Gwair part of the Betws mountain range, where he built himself a bungalow called Tor Clawdd and a laboratory complete with fifteen foot electrified fortifications. Paranoid or what! Oh and he also

had his own landing strip for his Gypsy Moth plane.
From there Harry began work on Aerial Defences for London, submarine detection apparatus and rockets powered by liquid hydrogen, this last idea was thirty-five years before Buzz Aldrin went to the moon in a liquid hydrogen powered spaceship. Then in 1938 he married Ganna Waleska, opera singer, perfumer and feminist whose four previous husbands had owned fortunes totalling $125, 000,000. After the nuptials she went on honeymoon on her own whilst Harry rushed back to continue his researches.

During his days at Tor Clawdd the locals were somewhat in awe of him apparently when he visited Clydach he always wore a long black coat, a black hat and of course the eye-patch, there is also an unconfirmed rumour of a meeting in the Masons Arms, Clydach between Harry and Sir Winston Churchill. Chris the current resident, pointed out to me a point where the road disappeared over the horizon which Harry apparently would train his binoculars on to see the owners of vehicles which he had knocked out with his "Death ray" desperately trying to restart with the hand-crank. Chris also pointed out to me the pond where Harry was supposed to have tested his radio controlled boats, the foundations of the laboratory are still there as is the place where Harry kept his Gypsy Moth which apparently had folding wings ----very James Bond.

When war broke out in"39" with Angela Merkel's lot the British Government were quite prepared to provide armed guards for Tor Clawdd and only last week I was delighted to discover that the father of a friend of mine who worked for the Post Office during the war, was given the job of "looking after" Harry; his father told him very little about Harry, possibly because he had signed the Official Secrets Act" but he did refer to him as a Boffin, a word that you don't hear nowadays very often..

Harry Grindall Mathews died in 1941 at Tor Clawdd of a heart attack and his friends had hardly finished scattering his ashes on "Mynnydd y Gwair before the War Department were going through his laboratory and taking away all his research notes and equipment.

And what happened to his plans for the Death Ray? I guess we will never know, they could be buried in a government vault, Harry could have destroyed them and taken their secrets to his grave or the more sceptical might think that he was exaggerating. His Pathé News reel certainly looks more Flash Gordon than it does NASA, but his Sky Projector must have worked and the British Government wouldn't have given £25,000 away for mere con and he demonstrated his Aerophone in front of the King, so I guess you pays your money and you takes your choice.

Steve Cound

LIMINALITY

This month for a change I want to talk about a word. I first came across this word in a book called "The Bardic Handbook" by Kevan Manwaring and it is a useful book for story tellers like ourselves and for people who want to learn about the Welsh Bard Taliesin and the Celtic Bardic traditions which are surprisingly healthy in Britain today And that word is liminal, L-I-M-I-N-A-L. It is a Latin word and means threshold. Pretty boring on its own but add a few prefixes and a suffix or two and you get in no special order:-

1. Limbo is taken from the Medieval Latin word limbus for hem or   border. And as any Catholic will tell you it is the mysterious lost border place between heaven and hell.

2. Liminal; Liminality can take many different forms:
    a) Liminality of time can refer to twilight which is the threshold between day and night. Apart from giving us beautiful sunsets,

it was the traditional time for mischief to be abroad in the forest and field and a time of fear for many young children whose mothers would have warned them " be home by twilight or the raggle-taggle gypsies'll have you or even worse, the fairies".

b) Or it can refer to dawn; An equally magical time, which for our ancestors meant that the black terrors of the night were over and a new day with new opportunities was beginning. It also involved another kind of liminality, that of states of consciousness, being on the threshold of a dream and waking and feeling the reality of it just slipping, slipping, slipping away.

c) A good example of liminality of place is an airport, the normal laws and jurisdiction of the country seem to be suspended at the check-in desk. Neither of the ground where they are located or of the sky, but some where in between and the people who inhabit them are also in Limbo from the same Latin root word. In a recent film Tom Hanks played an unfortunate character who was forced to live in an airport; not allowed to leave the airport because he had no visa, and neither could he return to his own country. One's sense of identity dissolves to some extent, bringing about disorientation.

d) Checkpoint Charlie was definitely liminal, a threshold between two hugely different cultures and societies.

e) Motorway service stations are liminal; they are such impersonal places because unlike a normal restaurant or cafe they seldom have a regular clientele just people on the move who may never call again.

f) At Christmastime, and during the winter solstice, Celtic and Western cultures use mistletoe, which since prehistoric times has been associated with magical ceremonies and is a plant that like the airport is neither of the ground or of the sky but inhabits a zone suspended between the two. And that plant, mistletoe is hung in a threshold or Limen and the act that occurs beneath it, between two people is a ritual ceremony, so that no taboos are broken. The word "Threshold" actually refers to the strip of wood placed on the floor in the doorways in Medieval times, so that the "Thresh" or Straw floor covering, was held inside the room

g) A crossroads has a particularly puzzling liminality, as you have three different thresholds or paths to choose from, yes! Oedipus [an adoptee and therefore liminal] met and killed his father at the crossroads and legend claims that Robert Johnson, the black American blues guitarist was at a crossroads, and at midnight when he is said to have sold his soul to the devil in exchange for his extraordinary talent, so liminality of time and place. Liminality can be sacred, alluring and dangerous.

h) Liminality of being exists particularly in creatures like caterpillars that can exist quite normally in one state and then undergo a transformation that seems nigh on miraculous, leaving behind a world of two dimensional travel in exchange for

> that of three dimensions. Tadpoles and frogs also go through a liminal phase. Wounds are liminal in that a wound is in constant flux, either getting better or getting worse. And in our own species, puberty is a liminal phase; neither child on the one hand nor adult on the other, neither one thing nor another. A time of mystery for friends and relatives who have no idea what the finished character will be or what changes large or small, will occur in voice, size, looks, or even talents.

Many social situations are liminal. Where the normal social groups or hierarchies break down and you are forced to mix with strangers from outside your social world.

During Chaucer's Canterbury Tales for example, The Miller told his bawdy tale alongside The Knight, The Merchant, and The Nun's Priest's tale. I have been spending a lot of time recently in the waiting room of the PDSA surgery and believe me when I tell you that I have seen the whole spectrum of society there, all united by a common concern for their pets. Definitely a liminal place.

3. Add a 'Sub' and you get   Subliminal:

Sub liminal also has mysterious and sometimes dangerous connotations. Sub liminal advertising is the sort where you don't even realise that you are being targeted. Whether it is the BMW or Dom Perignon 64 from a Bond film or the advertising running round the pitch during The Guinness 6 Nations Rugby Tournament, don't forget that word Guinness. It subtly weakens your resistance to those products and so the advertisers hope, weakens the purse strings when you see the product for sale. And then there is sub liminal conditioning or brainwashing. In some situations a hideous and illegal method of delving into the liminal part of the mind to plant responses to certain situations. Like in 1960's film The Mindbenders starring Dirk Bogarde and The Manchurian Candidate with Frank Sinatra.

4.   Swap the 'Sub' for a 'Pre' and you get Preliminary:

This can refer to some sort of early test or examination, to eliminate the ineligible or unsatisfactory or in medical terms to prepare the patient for what is to come, but again the sense is of being on the threshold of something, before the real thing.

Steve Cound

METAPHYSICAL POEM

Good Friday eve I didst betake
Myself to Summerhouse for to spake
On matters lofty and serene
And indeed Metaphysical e'en

And white I sat in Brown repose
My eyes they seem'd both to close
And thoughts didst soar untrammelled by
Earthly constraints. I was so high

That looking down I saw a stream
Chattering gaily all a gleam
That newly born into the world
Down through the rocks and crags it hurled

Just like a child set free from school
T'was no more governed by the rule
And free to choose it's own direction,
But looking back still felt connection

To the roots from which t'was sprung
In the days when it was young
But soon it reached a vale of tears
Equating to the teenage years

Throwing itself from cliff on high
Into the valley all awry
Trying to make its way in life
With rocks and rapids making strife

As it flowed down to the sea
It joined with others, one, two, three
Their currents gaily were entwined
As now the midday sun it shined

A broad, deep river that knew its place
Giving life and giving grace
Fertilising fields around
When it flooded o'er their ground

As the watercourse it slowed
Travelling over a smoother road
Meandering from side to side
In the valley that was so wide
It had collected towns about
It's banks, which prospered there no doubt
Then finally into the ocean
As a mark of its devotion

Joining with the mother of all
Heeding natures final call.

Steve Cound

PROSE POETRY; CASWELL

Last Saturday at Caswell Bay blue skies and golden sands water was warm for October I thought I'd take a chance.

The tide was nearly full in I set up in my usual spot close to the tap and the cafe; a handy wall nearby and behind me those rare peculiar plants that only know how to grow by the sea.

Forcing out of tiny cracks in the rocks so neat and just for me, as if the shoreline gardener had just finished and only now walked away.

Ignoring others I changed into my shorts well-practiced at that by now and eagerly made that swift short walk drawn by the call and the roar of the sea. The sea lapped round my ankles and calves, no problem thought I so far; then it reached up to the tops of my thighs and that familiar contraction occurred. Now the sea was up round my chest I could see that I wasn't alone, to my right the paddle-boards and the surfers doing their very own thing.

Surfability were down there too, giving disabled kids a ride; you strap them on, paddle them out and let them sail right in on the tide. To hear these paraplegic kids, laughing and shouting with glee. They may never, have experienced this before but they did so down by the sea.

Then with heart and senses full to the brim I know it's my turn to swim, but instead I lightly stir the water with finger and thumb and watch the drops fall broken by the sun into colours that have no name.

Finally I dive in and surrender myself to the ocean, for nothing, but nothing is bigger than this.

Steve Cound
18 November 2022

ZED'S HEAD

Zed's hair was ginger, naturally ginger, to the point of being orange in the summer and red in the winter. And having been blessed with it since birth and having two sisters similarly tressed and an uncle, he had kind of got used to it; all the cat catcalls in the school showers, the occasional comments on the street from strangers; "Oh! Ginge" and the looks of admiration and disbelief from those citizens of warmer climes who only ever saw black hair.

But today he was upset; his girlfriend had just split with him, oh, he had seen it coming these past few weeks, but she had actually called him a Ginger Whinger and it was all because of this lump on his shoulder. I mean he had taken it up to the doctor's who prodded it a couple of times. Looked at it learnedly and he had even stroked his chin; and then because he obviously didn't have a clue he said "Well, it could be a cyst, or a bursar or it could be even a ganglia. I'll put you down for a scan, you should receive an appointment in six to eight months, if you are lucky" he added cheerfully. Next!

He hadn't paid it much attention TBH, but then one day when he was shaving he noticed that that it was getting bigger and that it was growing hair and that the hair was black, now black in his family was about as common as a politician saying something sensible about Brexit to the long suffering electorate, in other words not, at all. In the days that followed his lump developed quite a dark thatch which spread down the sides and back, but strangely not across the front of the lump apart from two horizontal strips about an inch down from where the hair stopped.

He supposed, when he was telling me later on, that this should have given him a clue, but he was quite surprised taking one thing with another when what he had taken for pimples, started turning into eyes. I mean we are not talking about potato "eyes" now, these were the real McCoy eyelashes, pupils, eyelids, at least two on each eye not to mention the winking, and the blinking. Oh! And I forgot to mention the ears. Regulation issue ears, one pair, listening, for the use of.

Zed thought this was all great, he had been a bit lonely since Fiona left to tell the truth and now he had someone to talk to. And of course he was too well mannered to tell me, but what he realised was that his lump had no mouth, so it couldn't answer back. He could bore it to death and there was no way that it could get the hump [Oh! Zed chuckled at that pun] and leave like Fiona did.

So for the next few weeks Zed enjoyed the most lengthy and detailed conversations about the minutia of his life, and he could tell that his lump appreciated his words of wisdom by the way that it rolled it eyes understandingly at Zed's many trials and troubles, winked conspiratorially in the right places and even wrinkled its eyes up when Zed cracked a joke, which Zed swore was Lump laughing———-with no mouth.

Zed got the feeling that Lump was a bit sad and insulted at being called just "Lump" all the time, so one time in the shower he aimed the shower head at Lump's furry bonce and said "I hereby Christen you Lenny the Lump" and he swore that Lenny was so moved he saw tears of joy trickling from his eyes, of course it might just have been the water from the shower!

Steve Cound
27 October 2019

"A Trumpeter Swan greets his mate on a lake in Hickory Corners, Michigan." (Times photo)

Re-created on ply wood with Pyrography Pen.

Geraldine Edwards

A BYGONE STREET REMEMBERED

An ordinary street in South Wales in the 1950s. Just off the old A48, the part that is sandwiched between a mountain, a railway line and a steel works. And beyond that the sea. It was an unusual street, quite different to the others in the area as it had only one row of houses. We lived in the very end house at the bottom.

At the top to the left, stood an old farmhouse; the only remaining evidence of a farm which occupied the surrounding area before the land was sold off for housing back in the 1920s or 30s. There were also some outbuildings from where Will and Jinny (The farm) as they were known, ran a milk delivery business and sold fresh eggs which we often had for breakfast, lightly boiled with toasted soldiers, buttered with the best welsh salted. The toast by the way, was toasted on a toasting fork over the coal fire so we only had that in the cold weather.
The fireplace wasn't just a fire in a grate, it was a complete cooking unit with two wine coloured ceramic faced ovens, one above the other and two movable hobs, where a blackened kettle

seemed to be permanently on the boil or just simmering ready for the next pot of tea.

They, (Will and Jinny) had held on to a small L shaped piece of land which we called the field and this was bordered by a stream which we called the ditch which was far more appropriate. The ditch ran down the street opposite our houses and was lined with hawthorn trees and a barbed wire fence beyond. So all we kids had to do was open our front doors and cross the street, to climb, and catch tadpoles and tie bits of rope to branches in order to swing from one side of the ditch to the other. Until one day the rope or the branch, snapped, I can't remember which and Marian Jenkins (Jinx for short) in her very best party frock, white frilled ankle socks and shiny black patent shoes, landed with a huge splash, rising up from the muddy water covered in green slime looking like something out of one of those B horror movies. (I think she had to have a tetanus injection). Her mother was absolutely livid as she had specifically told her to change before she came out to play. Marian didn't live in our street, she lived on the main road.

At the top of the street on the right was Bevan's the shop. A hardware store, which sold everything and anything from Paraffin to Parazone (that's bleach to the uninitiated), from pop to paint, from wallpaper to washing soda and every size of screw or nail you could wish for. Joe and Annie the owners had two sons who, for some unknown reason, had a liking for climbing onto the roof. A pair of holy terrors they were. It was a common sight to see Joe, their Dad standing out in the street going red in the face, fuming, shaking his fist and shouting up at them to COME DOWN OR ELSE!

One day I was out in the garden and Marian Jenkins's mother was hanging out of her back bedroom window announcing to all that Annie had had a baby girl. I had no idea she was expecting.

I didn't even know where babies came from. But just accepted it without question. I must have only been about seven or eight but Annie used to allow me to wheel the baby up and down the street in her brand new silver cross pram. I loved it.

Now back to the bottom where we lived. Number 15. The O'Hagan's, (Rose and Patrick). Irish Catholics with seven children. Five girls and two boys. I was the youngest, a girl child. The baby, as I was always called. We were, along with number 13, a small three bedroomed semi-detached. The rest were terraced. Our house, was just a stones' throw away from the main Great Western, Paddington to Swansea railway line and beyond that was the steelworks. When we heard a train coming we'd race to the barbed wire fence and wave to the bewildered passengers staring out at us. A bedraggled bunch of snotty nosed ragamuffins just having fun. Some would wave back which pleased us immensely. Trainspotting was another pastime we enjoyed. Writing down the names and numbers of the various trains in little red note books. I can't remember any of the names but I do remember the Pullman looking very smart painted brown with yellow trim.

The steel works loomed large. There it was, huge and noisy, booming, banging, clanging, belching and spewing out steam and smoke and black dust which, to the annoyance of all the local housewives, settled on the window sills and their lines of clean washing. There were large flaming structures burning off excess gas which nowadays remind me of those giant transformer toys or a ferocious welsh dragon. I'd often lie awake at night watching through my window; the huge flames flickering and licking the night sky and lighting up my room making weird shapes on the wall.

My father was from Wexford and My mother was from Donegal but they met in America. New Jersey to be exact. Two of the many Irish emigrants who sought a better life and future for themselves in the land of endless opportunities. Had they stayed in Ireland they would never have met! However, the Great Depression hit, so Paddy came to join his brother Tom who was working on the building of the new docks. My father later went on to work in the steelworks as a crane driver for the rest of his life and hardly missed a day. My mother joined my father once he had established himself and they got married in St Joseph's Catholic Church. My mother was known as the American Lady as she wore clothes from New York fashion stores which were unavailable and definitely unaffordable to the local women. Eventually the clothes must have worn out and were replaced by floral wrap-around pinafores, but I do remember a beautiful full length night robe which hung on the back of the bedroom door. It was reversible, powder blue one side and pale pink the other. It had scalloped edges, and was made from high quality crepe. (Very Hollywood) I loved it and often dressed up in it, but never saw my mother wear it. I still don't know what happened to it? It just wasn't there anymore. So she ended up dedicating her whole life to us her children and family, making ends meet and ensuring we were all clean and well fed. I'm sure that wasn't the life she'd envisaged when she boarded that ship to America.

Next door to us were Mr and Mrs Lane and their daughter Jane. Jane was very glamorous and always wore the latest fashions. Mrs Lane had bright auburn hair worn in a French pleat and during the day whilst scrubbing her step and tiled front path, (which she always seemed to be doing) would wear brightly coloured chiffon scarves to keep it in place. Her nails were always painted red with lipstick to match and she wore Hedda Hopper style glasses. I cant remember much about Mr Lane, but apparently during the war, if you needed anything he was the go to. Anyway they moved away and Mr and Mrs Bowen moved in. They used to let me watch children's hour on their telly and had a dog called Tinker who became my best friend. Tinker was a beautiful black brown and white collie. As soon as I got home from school she would come calling at the back door for me to go out to play.

Next door to them at number 11 were the James's. Mr and Mrs James and their and granddaughter, Carol. Apparently Carol just turned up one day. I don't know what the circumstances were, but can only assume that they were, shall we say, complicated, and possibly sad. However, Carol was immediately accepted into the street and brought up by two loving grandparents and wanting for nothing. Mrs James was a seamstress and would often make our dresses. She even made wedding and bridesmaid dresses. I loved watching her work and hearing the crunch, crunch, sound of the scissors cutting through the paper pattern and cloth laid out on the table.

At number 9 were The McTavish's. (Scottish). Mr and Mrs McTavish, their daughter Evelyn and grandson Rodney. I used to play with Rodney when I didn't have anyone else to play with. He had a train set and lots of toys and always had a tube of Rowntree's fruit gums which were okay but I much preferred pastilles. Rodney's dad was nowhere to be seen but just turned up one day, 'out of the blue' as they say. Never did find out where he'd been. The mystery remains unsolved!

When the Council decided to build houses across the street, Rodney and I used to play on the building site. One day I climbed a ladder up to the first floor of one of the houses before they had fitted the staircase and he took the ladder away leaving me stranded. He just went home leaving me shouting "help! Help!" until my brother came and rescued me. I must have really pissed him off about something!

At number 7 were Mr and Mrs Daycock, (English). A genteel couple who kept themselves to themselves, as I remember it. Mr Daycock had been a medic in the First World War so whenever someone in the street needed first aid, Mr Daycock was the first port of call. I later found out that they'd lost their only son in the Second World War; I imagine they never got over it.

Next door to them at number 5 were Bevan's the Taxi. Mr and Mrs Bevan and their son Godfrey. Godfrey was, shall we say, very delicate and wore short trousers right up until he left school at fifteen. Mr and Mrs Bevan both looked very old to me and they both always wore black. They owned several taxis which were kept in garages on a plot of land just beyond our house, at the bottom of the street, before you got to the railway line. When I say garages they were more like big, black, giant tin sheds. We'd often see Mrs Bevan clambering up a ladder and scaling the roof with a bucket of tar to mend a leak, or lying under one of the taxis trying to fix an exhaust. You'd never see Mr Bevan doing anything like that. The taxis were, would you believe all Rolls Royce's; they even had a hearse. Big black monsters of cars they were. I assume now to have been 1940s models. Mr Bevan was very tall and very important looking and always kept himself to himself. Mrs Evans was so short that she would have to look through the steering wheel in order to see where she was going. They also had a daughter Erryl who went to live in London. I always thought she looked like Betty Grable. She married a Lord and had two children, Bronwyn and Robert who went to boarding school. They used to come and spend part of the summer holidays with Mr and Mrs Bevan whilst Erryl and hubby were holidaying in the South of France. Cannes I believe. So Erryl did very well for herself, thank you very much!

One of the highlights of the Summer was a trip to Porthcawl fair. Mrs Bevan would drive us in one of the Rolls Royce taxis. There would be me, Bronwyn, Robert, my sister Margaret, brother Michael, Marian Jenkins, Carol James and Kenneth and Newton Bevan. We were like something out of a Styx cartoon. Mrs Bevan peering through the steering wheel driving a Rolls Royce with nine kids in the back. All wanting a turn on the extra seats that you could pull out from the back of the front seats. You should have seen the looks on peoples' faces when a Rolls Royce rolled up, driven by a tiny old lady dressed in black with nine snotty-nosed kids tumbling out, all eager to get on the rides. My favourite was the trip around the world where you would get in a little boat and float around a series of tunnels which had depictions of places like Egypt and India. (I liked Mrs Evans). There are lots of entertaining stories about Bevan's the Taxi, too many to include here. Maybe another time. Well maybe one. I don't remember this but apparently Mr and Mrs Bevan had shares in a farm near Carmarthen and once a year they would go in a Rolls Royce and fetch a pig back for Will the farm to slaughter. Pork chops all round.

Next door to Evan's the Taxi at number 3, were Mr and Mrs Meyrick. I can't remember much about them except that they were related to Ivor Emanuel, who was a young man then and when he used to visit we would nag him to give us a song, which fair play he always did. He went on to become quite a successful singer and actor best remembered for his role as Private Owen in the film Zulu along with Stanley Baker and Michael Cain. His rendition of Men of Harlech in the face of the Zulu warriors is legendary.

Mr Meyrick caught us red handed, bobby knocking once. He must have been waiting behind the door.

At number one was Mr and Mrs Jinnifer. Mr Jinnifer was a policeman who we were all very afraid of and he had a big Alsatian dog which I was absolutely terrified of. I hated having to walk past that house.

So in a nutshell that was my street where every nationality of the British Isles and Ireland were represented, living alongside each other in harmony. With war heroes and characters and where lots of questions remain unanswered. If only we'd asked before.

Geraldine Edwards

Steve Ferris

THE HAZEL TREE
(Dappled Light)

Dappled light sun-drenched green leaf days,
Neighing deep threatened hoof thumping ways,
Stallions nipping necks on risen haunches,
Tensing rippling muscled thighs, eyes peering through branches.

Balmy afternoons spent squinting, sleeping,
Corrupted only by song thrush singing.
A glass of cool beer helped my dried up thinking,
Paper boy delivered chopped down printed forest
Journalist mission sometimes not so honest.

Dappled light lay here and ponder at man's madness,
To believe in this lake of life, is it Loch-ness?
Full of apparent helpless fervour for more of the same;
Cursed thoughts of mythical belief in fairies.
The "R" word hobbles minds no freedom to vary,
Constructed words, so say wisdom controlling people,
Projected sounds of minaret and lofty steeples.

Dappled light playing on the eyelids,
Ants on leaves nearby farming the aphids;
The afternoon quickly drawing to a close,
On highest perch the blackbirds song in repose.

Dappled light mirrored on river surface,
Dappled light deflects sun's rays intensity to purchase,
Across vole river his snout rippled wave,
This slight appearance that gives him away.

Banks interspersed with many different homes,
Willows dangled through surface water like combs;
Catching leaves 'nd crooked floating branches,
Poly-bagged hoards of jettisoned tranches.

Horses panting, magpies ranting, blackbirds singing,
Sparrows fetching, winging bringing, eating, chirping.

Dappled lights illuminate wisdom,
Open up minds trying to kill our kingdom;
Scattered light blurs normal senses,

Fortuitous bent carries on relentless.

The perpetrators of these four deeds,
Will one day find themselves in need.
"Come cry to us and shout for help,
Our master's ears brainwashed to pulp."
Imported wretched minds from other cultures,
Social experiments on this road gain punctures,
Awake our warriors who will fight off gloom,
Arrest the evil tide to our nation's doom.

Dappled light down long rooted fingers way,
Scrambled nights 'n' soldiers in those far off, hard-up days.
Little changes on the ranges of the battlefields to date;
Instead of trebuchet, these drones will bomb through windows on your plate.

Dappled light, sending the missionary to third world nations,
Followed by doctors to treat their sickly patients;
The arms dealers next to make security sales,
followed by commerce down industrialist trail.

Dappled light, certain degree of appeasement and subjugations,
Has to be imposed to educate another nation,
Dappled light if not for this, there'd be no fuzzy logic,
Dappled light; myths maybe I'll still believe in magic.

SJB Ferris

THE FRAGILE EARTH

What to do when the oil runs out,
Taken over by warlords with military clout,
Soldiers guarding the shops last pot of 'marmite',
Ransacked shelves just cannot be right.

We scuff hard shoulders from town to town,
Experience misery to make Facebook frown,
Hiding, woodland hoards, stripping orchard trees,
Stealing farmer John's honey, stung by his bees,

Cars, trucks 'nd bikers all out of fuels,
Government messages prove they've all been fools,
No pollutive gas trails from aircraft from the sky,
Give up wondrous gossamer winged iridescent damsel fly,

Seeking out shelter under the largest leaves
A tasty meal for a predator that may retrieve,
To those who appreciate nature's wonderful architecture,
Destroy it, never to experience Gaia's nectar.

SJB Ferris

DOWNSTREAM
The Crossroads

<u>Downstream</u>
Carry me downstream, floating, swimming in the river of life;
Willows piercing mirrored surface, reflections in dappled light.

<u>Downstream</u>
Two leaves curled in embrace, affections at their height,
Oxygen from carbon, their purpose liken man and wife.

<u>Downstream</u>
Swept by mysterious current from estuary across an ocean,
Under high tumultuous torrents, maybe naturally mixed up potion.

<u>Downstream</u>,
Landing far off shore, wind blown us to woodlands off the beach,
True love binding us together, our distant troubles cannot reach.

Downstream,
Winds of time blew these uniquely fashioned grains of stardust
Maybe if you believe in magic, these leaves love in tether rest in Gaia's crust.

Downstream,
Cooling for now, warming once the Pan god gave us paradise,
Now! Have we humans left it too late to for us realise?

Downstream,
Greed and more, drove man to maim his sister and mother,
This 'selfish gene' of madness brought him to kill his brother.

Downstream,
There his brain is bursting at the seams,
Blown apart all those family of dreams.

Downstream
The Greedy few with a speedy view on virgin lands and forest,

All taking pan's punishment for not being totally honest,

Downstream
Lessons to be learnt of 'needs' not 'wants', from the puffin and the gannet
Mankind's vast profits rocketing off to buy, not spoil another planet.

SJB Ferris

A JOURNEY OR JUST A DREAM

Weather fine, leisurely walk in the Cotswold on a winter's eve,
Then home for tea, seeing nature's best gently persuading them below
What more could one being need or in wanton lust desire,
Warming through 'nd through, prodding logs, good old English fire,
Yesterday eve we attended Iliad recital at Postlip Hall,
Hugh Lupton and Daniel Morden in poet skills gave their all,
If Darwen, Evans, Dawkins, Cook 'nd Scott sought those distant truths of life,
We may not able be so enlightened cutting religious myths, truths 'nd lies with a scientific knife.

Perhaps sail amongst the Hebrides or along our southern coast beyond,
To cruise passing wave torn rocks of Brittany's, famous river Gironde,
Taking a course around coast hugging Bay of Biscay,

Heading across the centre high risk in that wild affray!

Circumnavigating Santander 'n' Porto with Lisbon in our sights,
Waking at dawn, watching the city bathed in very special light,
All tired, main crew heads down to rest, well fed at last are we,
Two days hard sail we reach Trafalgar where the great Lord Nelson beat the Spanish,
We lay wreaths to both nations, sailors where they fought bravely, saw their daylight vanish.

Heading for Barcelona and the Costa's our onward make,
To grab some real sunshine for Gilly, Frances and Johanna's good sake,
Hope that Andy 'nd Claire, Mike 'n' Alison on Rainbow seeker,
Andy 'n' Claire are not seasick with taking over, not feeling weaker,
The rock of Gibraltar in our sights,
Claire reported on radio with delight,
Andy stood up, started frantically clapping,
The boat turned upwind sails a-frapping.

I picked up the radio mic calling up to speak to Claire,
Asking her to take to the wheel if she really dare.
Claire jumped at the chance
Crossed deck, leaping over obstacles in a frantic dance.

In my rush to take on the steering,
I knocked Andy overboard who started screaming!
"Where's the life sling?" Alison asked,
"either side on the rails abaft."

Andy was hanging off the edge of the ladder,
We pulled him aboard. He couldn't be gladder.

Good job my life jacket's on right,
Mike checked the straps were all tight.
Tell them what happened to Andy, no time to relax
Next time, make sure safety lines attached.

So with both crews gathered in Gibraltar, Shepherds Marina Quay,
Tomorrow Algeciras, road trip in Spain there we'll be,
We toured several towns and villages, then back to Gibraltar we went,
Dared not check our account balances for all the money we'd spent;
We had a party aboard the Rainbow seeker,
Then we returned to our boat to sleep on Dreamer.

SJB Ferris

GREED AND BELIEFS

Godforsaken, not forsaken everyone's a winner,
He'll provide for you when you can't afford your dinner,
God is all, he's all the answers, but will he let you know?
Will he refuse to allow man's minds to free thoughts and to grow,
Or will he watch while killers creep to obliterate you in numbers,
To carry on with blinkered mind is it worth to be so encumbered,
Energy, food, materials, sources fought for o'er the world in man's blind faith he blunders.
Thinks he's managing just OK; really controlled and appeased by the power mongers.

Godforsaken man with his godforsaken empty oil can for the future he has no plan
Perhaps God's will have the answer, more likely who's left in hope will all return to Pan.

SJB Ferris
07.05.11

Frances Susan Gardner

MYSTICS CAVERN CORNER

Where birds fly high for fear of their very own wish bone,
becoming extrapolated, along with their balls;
for the mystics, spell pot, found ever on the boil;
then next the wise old Rats.
Running for the sake of their toenails,
and the tips of their ears,
as an ancient knowledge they have, of the mystics' brew.
They whisper to each other, there is no way to change life,
but we will all get by, so look at it wisely and straight in the eye;
then look again.
Maybe these mystics have magic to share,
so we won't be upset, only aware.
They're different to us;
their encounters will not be the same,
and nor are the words that they come with,
then they are not to blame.
So welcome their smile and welcome them in;
see then, what they have to bring.

Frances Susan Gardner

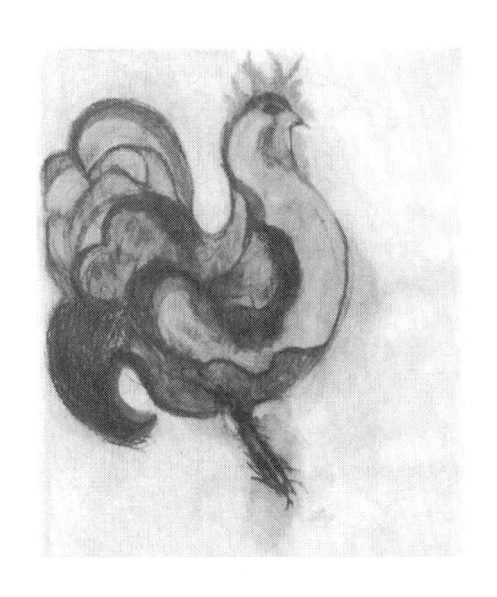

'Cock-A-Loo'
Felt tip pens on 80gm plain paper.

TRICK OF THE MOON

Trick of the moon, you're a mean old man,
Playing around because you can.

How dare you chuckle
Chuckling at your wizardry.
Mean old man
Playing around because your can.
The hell with you, with your spite.

She was on a freedom road
when you saw her there;
The cards had been read
only hours before –
many things she saw.
She didn't believe it to come true,
but smiled to herself, a wishful fool.
The moon was full and mean that night,
Trick of spite because you can.

Trick of the moon, you're a mean old man,
You spread intrigue, a deadly road,
The unexpected you surely wove,
there was only a *prince* that became a toad.
Huh! Trickster -

Trick of the moon;
Silver night,
Full of spite,

There was only a prince,
That became a toad
At the end of that road
Trick of the moon,
A bad mean old man.

Frances Susan Gardner

'Mr Peck'
Eye shadow & nail polish on watercolour paper.

'You can keep your hat on'
Pencil drawing.

Jane Harrison

'Garden flowers on Easel'
Acrylic on paper.

'Marooned shell'
Watercolour on paper.

Still Life Composition'
Acrylic on canvas.

M.B Howell

A LAST MINUTE HOLIDAY TO SRI LANKA

Travelling with a friend, no time for our tickets to be posted and told we were to pick up our tickets two days later at the Hayes & Jarvis desk, Heathrow Airport, to catch our flight to Sri Lanka. Both excited at our opportunity for our cheap seven night stay in Sri Lanka. At the same desk picking up their tickets, were a father and mother, plus their two boys and a family of three; a single mum with her teenage son and daughter. It turned out we were all heading for Sri Lanka and we ended up on the same transfer coach, all booked into the same hotel. We bonded and are still friends to this day.

The hotel staff were amazing as were all the Sri Lankan people. A basic hotel, good food, entertainment in the evening, and the swimming pool was fantastic, overlooking the sea. All nine of us together visited Beruwala, where there was an amazing Buddhist Temple; we had a ferry from the hotel and on the way back we had a Tuk Tuk race back to the hotel.

My favourite person we met at the hotel was Kuma, a special man who had a twelve seater people carrier, who offered us, and all nine accepted, his overnight excursion to Kandy, taking in the Sri Lankan traditional dance show, visiting the tea plantations, the Elephant Orphanage, Elephant Safari and washing the Elephants in the river with coconut shells. We also visited the amazing Mount Sigiriya, an ancient rock fortress and walking to the top was worth it for the views and especially seeing the 5th century paintings of the concubines.

Our trip was wonderful, however, five years later, on Boxing Day, 26th December 2004, Sri Lanka was hit by the Tsunami and I often wonder and pray if Kuma and his family are safe.

MBH

Anne Marie

'Giraffes' in Love'
Terracotta clay, triple-glazed.

Annette Nash

UNSUNG HERO

He was full of bravado and showed no fear,
as he swung into town with all his gear,
A gun on each hip and his bandoleer.

The quarry was an outlaw called Fearsome Fred,
Whom the townsfolk had all come to dread.
Into the saloon he confidentially swaggered,
Fred's face suddenly looked rather haggard.

"Stick em up, Fred, I've got you covered."
But Fred was too quick he dived into a cupboard.
Our hero, disconcerted, tripped and fell,
and all that was heard was a scream and a yell.

As a myriad of crystals fell into the beer,
'Oh my, Oh my', he's shot the chandelier;
The place erupted and people ran amok,
As chaos consumed all those who were struck.
By the fine smithereens of the fine chandelier,
our hero was wishing that he could disappear.

Fred made an appearance and people heard him jeer,
"Call yourself a hero! I'm over here!"

But our hero was gone, covered in shame,
and to crown it all found his horse was lame.
Slinking off into the sunset, full of despair,
Wishing he'd never shattered that chandelier.

Annette Nash

Claire Rozario

'Good Morning World'
Watercolour and acrylic on paper.

MY FEATHERED FRIEND

"Look, Grace, do you see them. Up on the wire, two birds right there?"

Grace looked out of the small hospital window onto a residential street. She could see nothing. She studied the pylon with its spidery tendrils looping across the houses, but there were no birds. She turned back to Bill as a black thundercloud exploded and heavy rain started to hammer down. "Sorry love, I can't see them." She said. "There!' he exclaimed, wild with excitement, right there!"

Humouring him she said, "Oh yes, Bill, I see them. Magpies. One for sorrow, two for joy." She smiled kindly.

"Grace, they're Crows, not Magpies! Look at their oily feathers and their beady eyes, glassy and polished like marbles. They've been watching me for days."

Bill had been lying in his bed in the hospital for nearly three weeks, and recently he seemed to be losing his grip on reality. Mr Wray, the Consultant, re-assured Grace that hallucinations were quite common in cases like these and he had, after all, suffered a terrible fall.

She left the hospital feeling sad and helpless. She drove the short distance home through pouring rain as persistent blue flashes of electricity rampaged through the sky, accompanied by the deep sounds of rumbling thunder. She was relieved to finally bump her car up the driveway.

Just before 6.00 o'clock her mobile rang. "Mrs Jackson, we have a situation. Please can you come to the hospital." Arriving there fifteen minutes later, Grace was surprised to see Bill's bed flanked by an army of doctors and nurses. Bill's bed however was empty, and she shot the Consultant a confused look. "I'm afraid your husband seems to have vanished." He spoke solemnly. Just then she saw him. Through the window a small figure was edging its way across the roof, making slow progress against the elements. Grace screamed. "Good God it's Bill. He's on the roof." she clasped her hand over her mouth. The rain was still pelting down, and a fork of lightning ricocheted its way across the sky, blasting through the black clouds and yet Bill continued his journey on slippery tiles. "It's those damned bloody birds." Grace said, fixing her gaze at the strange sight.

On the roof, Bill was sliding towards his goal. "Nearly got you, demons," he said, inching closer. When he eventually reached the summit, he leant precariously out towards the wire taking wild swipes. An almighty crash of thunder startled him, and he almost fell, but he clung on, never losing focus. Clambering back up, he stood like a sublime effigy; saturated in sweat with his striped pyjamas and dressing gown almost transparent against the elements. He was cursing amid sobs, exhausted; a broken man. All at once Bill caught the tail end of another flash of lightning and fell to a seated position and as he stood up again another bolt hit him right between the eyes. At this, his body plunged off the edge and the chord from his dressing gown lodged on the weathervane. Like some macabre play, Grace and the medical team could only watch in horror as Bill's blackened body was whipped around like a demonic rag doll; his grey hair standing out in frazzled peaks. Grace screamed and fainted.

That was six weeks ago. Grace still hadn't fully got to grips with the tragedy although her teenage daughter Kate has been a marvellous tonic. "Philosophically," she said "If it wasn't all so tragic, Dad would've enjoyed that. Talk about going out in style." "I thought you were gonna say like a light then." Said Grace half smiling. "To be fair though Mum, as an electrician, it was quite a fitting end."

Grace got up to draw the curtains. She turned to Kate, "Do you see that bird on the line? I'm sure it's been watching me ever since Dad…" she trailed off. "You mean the Magpie, Mum…one for sorrow?" "It's not a Magpie, it's a Crow." Grace corrected her.

Minutes later they heard Esmeralda's low growl outside the backdoor. The tell-tale sound of a killer. "Oh, here we go." Said Grace, as Esmeralda swished through the cat flap and dropped the biggest blackbird she had ever seen on the kitchen floor. "Oh God! Take that outside, vile creature." Grace screamed, "I don't want to see any more dead things."

Esmeralda eyed her for a second and then wandered off, discarding her kill like it was yesterdays news. She paused to lick the underside of her front leg, then hopped onto the sofa to continue the body wash. "God's perfect killing machine." said Kate, "Gross!" Grace bent down to sweep up the bird and couldn't help noticing its odd shaped beak. "Looks like it has a Roman nose," said Grace, "how funny." "What like Dad's you mean?" said Kate amused. Grace turned the bird over and then gasped in horror. On the other side of the beak was a triangle-shaped scar. Grace gasped "The boating accident in France, Kate it's him, it's Dad," she cried in horror, "look at the scar on his beak!" She rushed to the back door, flung it open and ran outside looking left and right. The bird on the fence had gone. "Kate, where are the birds, where are all the birds?" Kate followed her outside. "Mum, you're right; they're gone." They walked back inside and froze. The dead crow was now human sized and very much alive. He sat nonchalantly at the kitchen table, his legs crossed. "Hello Grace," it chirped, "I finally managed to catch one of those birds. You were right, they were Magpies after all. One for sorrow."

Claire Rozario

NIGHT TRAIN

I was on the night train to Hell. Flames, like fiery autumn leaves rushed up along the sides of the track, licking at the windows as we headed deeper and deeper into the black. Tunnels barely visible swamped us and grey fog swept through the carriage creating vast eerie shadows, ten feet tall. The man opposite coughed in the fumes and his chubby face turned red. 'I can't breathe.' He mouthed, fumbling for his handkerchief. 'Open the window!' I shook my head solemnly. 'We can't let them in!' He paused mid cough, "Can't let who in?" he asked, confused. "The night demons." I smiled, ambiguous, knowing, "Didn't you get the memo?"

Suddenly there was a furious tapping at the window and the man jumped and fell back into his seat; the train's whistle blasted a warning. The hammering, repetitive and chilling continued, more urgent now, more disturbing somehow and then the finale; a long, ear-splitting screech of nails being dragged across the glass. Then nothing. No faint whisper.

Absolute. Nothing. The man sighed, wiped his brow with his handkerchief and folded it back into his top pocket. He picked up his flask and carefully removed the lid, relaxing fractionally.

I had a vial; a small potion for my transition. I hadn't used it yet. It wasn't time yet. This was just the start; this was just the warm-up. As if picking up my thoughts, the train started shuddering and gathering speed. Faster and faster it went, rampaging across country, ricocheting wildly, bouncing impossibly; like a de-railed fairground ride. The man fixed small rigid eyes on mine. His flask fell clanking to the floor and then shunted off a couple of seats before finally settling itself under the adjacent table. A mixture of terror and excitement rushed through my veins and I smiled as I let the frenzy take control. It was nearly time. Bright flashes of red and yellow dotted the chamber and then disappeared again like fireworks. I closed my eyes and then opened them again abruptly as the dividing door suddenly swung open revealing the great frame of the ticket Inspector. Everything about him was pristine. His perfectly pressed uniform, his polished buttons, his shiny shoes. His imposing figure stood like a ghostly waxwork. The train juddered on relentlessly, but the ticket inspector didn't move. Not a twitch. Not a flinch. Not a muscle. He cast a dark shadow over my companion. "Tickets please." He said.

The man whined and a sweat broke out on his forehead. "B-b-but I don't have a ticket." He looked at the Inspector, unsure, then at me. The Inspector spoke softly, but his voice was crystal clear above the clattering of metal. Somehow. "Oh, I'm sorry sir, then you'll have to get off." With that he flung open the door and tossed him outside like a bag of rubbish. The door slammed shut. He turned to me and smiled. "It's almost time." he said.

The train began to slow and was now no more frenzied than a light breeze. It started gracefully cruising to a stop. The breaks screeched, crunching metal against metal and then it gave its final shunt and stopped.

"Were we finally here? Was this Hell?" It was still so black I couldn't see any difference and I felt disappointed for a second. 'What were the rules? Was anyone coming to take me on to the next step of my initiation?' The carriage door swiftly opened, and a gentle voice drifted into my consciousness.

"Hello, Sir, it's time to get off." I glanced in the direction of the voice and saw that it belonged to an elderly rail guard. His skin, like his immaculate uniform, was grey, his complexion gaunt, pallid; his eyes the palest blue. He smiled distantly.

"Is it time now?" I enquired. "Oh yes sir, I would say it's definitely time now." He held the door open. "If you'd like to come with me, I will escort you to the rest of your party." "Have I arrived in Hell?" I had to ask. "Yes, Sir; you have arrived safely in Swindon. I hope you had a good journey."

As I looked past the guard, I spotted four men I recognised from the Sales Team. I reached inside my breast pocket and pulled out my vial, only it wasn't a vial, it was a large bottle of Paracetamol. The guard smiled again, "These team building weekends, really take their toll don't they Sir?"

Claire Rozario

THE TAILOR AND THE THIEF

On a cold night, you can often see the light burning brightly in the old post office on the corner of Gryphon Street. Now home to *The Tailor*, Julius Carver, affectionately known as Mr Stitch, its once shabby interior, the cracked slate floor tiles, the woodworm-decayed counter and rows of dusty shelves had all been transformed. Spotlights now shone onto brightly painted shelves on which were stacked rolls of the most delectable fabrics. Iridescent taffeta, oil-slick satin, if you could see it in your imagination, you would surely find it amongst the stock. Large glass jars brimming with exotic beads and sparkling sequins lined up in rows against boxes of trinkets and unusual findings. All bearing black labels with perfect gold italics. Hanging above the front window, a colourful curtain of ribbons rustled and crinkled on their oversized silver hooks. Most nights Mr Stitch would work his fingers into the small hours and like a surgeon, he operated with deft precision. Stitching pearls onto ball gowns, tacking perfectly straight white stitches around a gentlemen's suit lapel, and rich sumptuous velvets he laced with such delicate silk threads you'd think they were spun by a spider. Costumes for the exceedingly rich, that held secrets you would never believe. Mr Stitch kept a locked cupboard of the finest glass vials and in them, he kept the souls of the dead and these souls he sewed into the seams of every garment.

Tony Grainger, Sports Personality of 1982, had recently lost his wife, and after 6 lonely months had decided to treat himself to a new suit. As he stood in front of the mirror in Mr Stitch's parlour, turning to admire the finish, he was impressed. It was a perfect fit and so exquisitely sculpted. "Can I touch it?" he spoke to his reflection, jerking his thumb in the direction of the pocket. "Oh yes,£ said Mr Stitch, "I suggest you keep a silk handkerchief in there and that way you can blot your forehead if you need a boost." Tony smiled, his eyes shiny with emotion. "Maybe I'll take up painting again once Ena has taken hold." "Very good Sir.'" Mr Stitch replied. Auntie Ena was Tony's beloved Aunt. She had been gone for twenty years but he had never forgotten her. She was the artist of the family, the one who painted beautiful beachscapes in oils. She wore bright red lipstick, always, and had hypnotised more than a few men in her day. She was vivacious with a big kind heart and her spirit was now neatly sewn into the breast pocket of a blue and grey Harris Tweed jacket. Tony wore the garment proudly and left the shop in a flurry of excited thank-you's. Mr Stitch watched him walk away, stopping a few yards from the house to tilt his hat and gaze into the middle distance. He made that shape with his hands that artists do when looking at perspective. Mr Stitch smiled down at the grey tabby cat sitting on the windowsill. "We will make the unhappy, happy again." He declared as he smoothed the fur on the cat's head.

Mr Stitch had moved into 21 Gryphon Street exactly three hundred and fifty-one days ago. Exactly two weeks before Christmas day; exactly one week before little Molly Madden was to become a year older and exactly one week before a terrible history was to be created.

Molly Madden was the doctor's daughter, a whirlwind of energy, very popular at school and, although God knows how with the constant chattering, always top of the class with exceptional grades. Noisy child. But she had something about her, and Mr Stitch had something very special for her. He had been keeping the soul of her dear departed Grandma Cilla for 2 years, waiting for the right time to pass her on. Molly would be eight years old in one week and Mr Stitch thought that was a very good age. The magical number eight. Mr Stitch would design the most splendid dress for her party with a little pinch of grandma and her wisdom sealed inside the cushioned buttons down the front. Mr Stitch found the measurements for Molly's dress and then walked across the red tiled floor and into the parlour. He unlocked the cupboard and stared at the bank of vials, all carefully labelled with the same perfect italics. The vials seemed to breath in unison and it created a strange calm. He picked up a red bottle bearing the name Alice Brown. Ah dear Alice he thought, that brilliant writer, I shall enjoy using you when Joshua is old enough. He put the bottle back. Another bottle jumped from the shelf; it was labelled 'Ga..ma illa' It was a dark blue bottle. He frowned. Not his neat script. He scratched his head. "But it must be." He said to himself, shrugging. He carefully locked the cupboard up and walked back to the front of the shop. He gazed at the stacks of material, trying to find something to compliment his design. His eyes settled on a pale peach satin right on the top shelf. He had just opened the back door to fetch a ladder, when the sound of heavy boots dropping onto the concrete caught his attention. The man was dressed entirely in black. Only the whites of his eyes were showing, and he was carrying a black rucksack. Mr Stitch didn't flinch. "'h Jim, just the person, can you take this ladder in for me, and then you can show me what's in your bag."

Mr Stitch's nephew, Jim, worked in the family Undertaker's. He was an expert thief, and the stealer of souls. He caught the souls just at the time they separated from their bodies and he corked them like fine wine into the small bottles. The bodies would then be incarcerated forever in their final resting place, beneath a nailed casket. Timing is everything, but Nimble-fingered Jim, as he was known locally, was the best in the business.

This curious little enterprise worked like a charm for many years, but of course nothing lasts forever, and it does not come without pitfalls. Sometimes bad things happen; very bad things. What happened on that Christmas afternoon just after the Queen's speech, went down in history for all the wrong, despicable, tragic reasons.

The headline in the morning's Gazette read:

'Molly Madden, 8, Eats Cake Amid Killing Spree!'

Just after Molly blew out the candles on her enormous cake, she made a wish. "What's your wish, darling?" her mother, Jilly, asked. "I wish you were all dead!" She said, before picking up the carving knife and thrusting it with force into the eye of Tommy Brady. He didn't have time to react before he fell to floor and lay perfectly still with thick blood oozing its way out of his empty socket. Molly laughed. "Who's next?" she taunted as children began crying and screaming and clambering away. Chelsea James didn't run; she was too horrified. Molly turned to face her.

"It must be you!" she deftly slit her throat from ear to ear and then wiped the knife on her beautiful iridescent dress. She hacked of a piece of cake and ate it greedily. Her father tried to approach gently, but she sliced through the sleeve of his favourite mauve sweater and drew blood on his forearm. Tim yelped and Molly ran towards the front door. "Nobody's going anywhere," she said picking off Catherine Rogers and Dexter Jones in quick succession. "It's my party and everyone will do as I say." She turned on her cousin Davy. "Stop crying, baby," she said plunging the knife full tilt into his neck. "Sooo annoying!"

In the background to this chaos, the six adults were watching it all happen in slow motion. The police were been called, but it would be another full hour before the carnage stopped. It took Molly's father and two large policemen to finally wrestle the weapon out of her hands. With Molly clawing and biting, Jilly managed to strip the dress off her. In an instant Molly reverted from savage assassin to small terrified child. Molly killed fifteen of her friends, including her two cousins. She's so traumatised she hasn't stopped screaming since. "It's a disaster, an atrocity, a tragedy, a horror story," Jilly cried to Mr Stitch the next day. "What have you done?" Mr Stitch was genuinely alarmed. He realised immediately what must have happened. After consoling the Madden's he went in search of Jim to ask him a few pointed questions. The thief was too nimble for Mr Stitch and he had darted out the back door and disappeared into the crowd shortly after hearing the harrowing tale. It would be a long day before he would come crawling pitifully back asking for forgiveness. When he did finally surface, he was full of apology and begged forgiveness. He admitted that he had dropped his bag and two of the bottles were unlabelled. He found one label and put it back on but had to write out the other one in his own hand. He knew they were similarly named souls, but he just couldn't remember which was which. "Grandma Cilla was one," said Mr Stitch, "but who was the other one?" Jim looked about, sheepish, couldn't look Mr Stitch in the eye. "It was," he said and then stopped, "It was," he started again. '" think it was a Gangnam Killer." I'm so terribly sorry.

A week later, there was an unexpected snowstorm. It was like all the world's snow had fallen in one night. It had settled right up to the letterboxes and everyone was marooned. Forced to eat yesterday's bread and get on with those boring tasks around the house, there was no celebrating New Year's Eve tonight and by 9 o'clock everyone took to their beds with extra quilts and steaming mugs of cocoa. Even Mrs Quinn's chickens were confused by the weather and had all but buried themselves under straw bundles and were cosying down for proper winter. The next day it was much warmer, and the snow had gone, in fact there wasn't a trace of it to be seen anywhere. Like stepping into a parallel universe, where things are familiar but strange. Stranger still was the sudden absence of the old post office. Mr Stitch's neat home had simply vanished into thin air. The plot that was once a colourful Pandora's box of charm, was now just an empty space with a small tin shed leaning against the house next door. A note was pinned to the front of the shed. It simply said 'Gone Away.'

Claire Rozario

THE EDGE OF LIFE

Old Ed, sat on the porch swigging beer, rocking. Swigging and rocking. Looking way, way past the sun.

Locked. Loaded. Ready. A long time ready.

Claire Rozario

THE DAWN OF THE RATS

Everybody loves the sound of a train in the distance, unless you know it's not really the sound of a train, just a hollow ghostly sound, something remembered from a dream; from a place far away, long ago; a powerful hallucination, significant by its absence.

Jett tilted his head and squinted out from the wide brim of his Stetson. One of the last remaining relics from the other world; it never left his head. It's battered hide, sun-bleached and comfortable, was a permanent reminder. Stitched into the brim were a series of tiny electrodes, links to their world, not his. Electric waves of energy were pin-pricked, undetected, into the base of his skull twice a day as knowledge, but not as we know it, was streamed into his core. It kept him apart from the others. It was his secret link to the other world, and nobody knew about that. He'd traded his horse for a motorcycle in the millennium, when the last of the bikers cruised through the portal between life and death. It was just a rat bike essentially, but it blended where he couldn't.

Sand brushed over his boots and the hot desert sun bounced off the dull metal of the chopper, blowing dust clouds into the air. From his viewpoint, miles and miles of desert lay ahead, and he could still hear the train somewhere clattering over wooden rafters, pushing against metal as it rattled down the track. He adjusted his hat and slipped one hand inside the pocket of his jeans. He pulled out a dog-eared photograph and studied it, tracing his finger across the image of the beautiful girl in the yellow sundress. He wanted to weep. She was such a fragile memory. This wasn't the time and he had work to do.

He was a rat. Not physically, like the others, but, by definition. He was a farmer in the old world and despite appearances, he was British. You'd be right to think he was brought up in the place though, with his long, dirty blonde hair scratched back into a ponytail, the stolen aviators. He had the look of a cattle rancher or lonesome cowboy. How could he not fit right in?

He found the hub by accident. Before the bikers came, he was travelling through somewhere, it was hard to tell now as there was a vast emptiness about the place. He could have been anywhere. His bike had dipped in the dunes and he stopped to check for damage. That's when he noticed the tiny pulse of violet light coming from under the sand bush. He traced the thin line further underground and then he slipped in the flimsy covering and found himself in an underground chamber surrounded by archaic machinery. It was not monitored and there were no cats. He wasn't going to hang around for long. Tinkering about with electronics in his gap year as a roadie gave him some basic understanding. It wasn't solid, but in a short time he fashioned a crude device using his insulin needles as a carrier and created a small charge that would, he hoped, turn him invisible for short periods. Long enough, he hoped, to close the gap on the cat people. There was nothing he could do for his wife Elvira, she was fully cat now and no longer had any human traits, but he could at least try to figure out a way to save the other rats before she ordered the destruction of what was left of the planet. Elvira, was now the Queen of this planet and he had to kill her. His next move would be crucial.

He climbed onto his chopper, and waited for a moment, listening to the low throb of the engine. The purring reminded him of home, the place he was not very far removed from. He wasn't looking forward to killing his wife, but it was a necessary step he had to take. He was a rat that wasn't going down without sinking the ship first.

Claire Rozario

'Yungblud'
Acrylic on canvas.

Gina Smith

'Storm on the Horizon'
Watercolour on paper.

Mike Witchell

GLYDE

Willie and Ginny are enjoying their very first date. Willie is doing the talking.

"So, how did you enjoy the hors d'oeuvre, babe? Would you like a little touch more, or shall we move on to the main?"

"I'm more than ready for the main if you are."

"Two secs, and I'll be with you. Don't go away now."

He leaves the room and returns moments later.

"Here we are. I'll just, er . . . unless you'd care to?"

"No, no, you carry on. No, wait. It is vegan, isn't it?"

"Vegan! What do you mean vegan?"

"I'm serious," Billy.

"It's Willie, actually."

"Well, I'm serious - Willie. If it's not vegan, forget it."

"Oh what? I've never even heard of vegan . . . you're not joking me, not just winding me up? It's not some kind of meat gag, is it?"

"No, it's not some kind of meat gag. Meat for me is no laughing matter. I've been vegan now for, let me see, nearly six whole . . .

"Six whole years – wow! I'm impressed."

"Six whole days – and I mean proper vegan. Plant based. Totally plant based."

"Yes, but . . ."

"Willie, I'm not one of these people who say they're vegan, and then two minutes later you see them putting whole milk in their Americano. Pathetic, they are, sodding vegetrendians. If I choose to do something, I do it full on . . ."

"Full on, eh? I like the sound of that."

"Yeah, like literally full on. So I'm off milk, eggs, chicken, fish, honey . . ."

"Meat. Come on, Ginny, it's not like it's a bacon buttie."

"We'll have to check, that's all. It is out of a packet, I take it."

"'Course it's out of a packet."

"So, is it vegan or not?"

"I don't know if it's vegan. I didn't stop to look. It's not as if I bought it - I borrowed it off my flatmate. My flatmate Johnny."

"Borrowed it? Are you going to give it him back then?"

"Ha-ha. At this rate, probably yes."

"Look, you must still have the packet. If the packet says vegan, that's good enough for me."

"Packet! The packet's in the bin. Some brand I've never heard of it was."

"Well, be a good boy, and go fetch. Please. Pretty please."

"Okay, okay."

"Well?"

"Glyde, it is. That's what it's called, Glyde. Glyde with a y. Got a stupid flower on the box. It's a new one on me."

"I can see that, Willie boy. Question."

"What now?"

"Is your pal Johnny a vegan?"

"Dunno. Never asked. Subject's never come up."

"Well his condoms are vegan. Glyde are the only vegan condoms you can get. So it's your lucky day, thanks to Johnny. Now come here, you."

"Question."

"Well?"

"Will this count as one of my five a day?"

Mike Witchell
Tapestri, Discovery Room
November 2019

WHAT'S SAUCE FOR THE GOOSE . . .

"It's not funny, dear, it's goosist. Turn it off at once, please."

Mother Goose was not amused by the latest repeat of TV's Fawlty Towers. Not amused at all. Basil Fawlty's goose step had always ruffled her feathers, and it enraged her even more to hear the goslings' gleeful guffaws at the celebrated "Don't mention the war" episode.

"Oh, mum," they chorused, but she was adamant. Bungling Basil was cut off in mid sentence.

"Don't mention the . . ." screeched the highly strung hotelier.

"Goose step," hissed gosling Bruce. "Don't mention the goose step."

Too late he spoke, too late.

"It's not as if us geese even do the ghastly goose step," grumbled Mother Goose.

"You never see one goose standing on one leg, let alone a whole gaggle of us. We'd fall over if we so much as tried. So why call what has become a byword for human militarism and dictatorship after us?

"Goosism, that's why. Goosism pure and simple. You take a gander at the eagles – their record over the years is nothing short of a disgrace, but no-one holds that against them."

"Hotel Californa? It's a bit dated but it's not all that bad," said young Bruce Goose, her eldest son.

"Not those eagles – I mean the ones with wings," snapped his mother. "The eagle has been used as a heraldic motif by every tyrant from the Romans to the Romanovs, not to mention Franco's Spain and Nazi Germany, but no-one has a bad word for eagles.

"Protected species, your eagle, for all its evil connotations. And humans don't talk of eagling one another, oh no! Goose one another, that's what they do when they tweak some unsuspecting bottom, another vile slur on us.

"Then there's gooseberries, that's another thing. Why goose? We don't eat the hairy green horrors, but it's our name they've been given. Brings me out in goose bumps just to think of it.

And playing gooseberry. Don't get me started on that."

Desperate for his mother not to get started on that, Bruce makes a bold but fateful decision to turn on the radio. A reading from the Renaissance writer Rabelais is just drawing to a close.

"I have, said Gargantua, by a long and curious experience, found out a means to wipe my bum, the most lordly, the most excellent, and the most convenient that ever was seen."

The goslings were agog! Bottoms on Radio Three!

"I maintain that of all torcheculs, arsewisps, bumfodders, tail-napkins, bunghole cleansers and wipe-breeches, there is none in the world comparable to the neck of a goose that is well downed, if you hold her head betwixt your legs.

"Believe me, you will thereby feel in your nockhole a most wonderful pleasure, both in regard of the softness of the said down and of the temperate heat of the goose.

"And think not that the felicity of the heroes and demigods in the Elysian fields consisteth either in their asphodel, their ambrosia or their nectar, but in this, according to my judgment, that they wipe their tails with the neck of a goose, holding her head betwixt their legs."

Mother Goose never listened to the radio again.

"Goosism," she spluttered; "Goosism is so ingrained in the human mind that trying to avoid it is . . . is . . . "

"Something of a wild goose chase?" Bruce suggested helpfully.

Mike Witchell

LADDER

It's a man's world, the land of the ladder, a world of window cleaners, firemen, steeplejacks and peeping toms.

Almost the only time you see a woman on a ladder is when she is being carried down one by one of the aforementioned males. Fortunately for her, usually there is the whiff of smoke in the air.

Firemen, of course, are on the top rung in the popularity stakes where ladder men are concerned, dashing heroes envied by men and desired by women - or vice versa, depending on taste.

Not so the humble window cleaner, with his bucket and scrim, and as for steeplejacks – well, put it this way: when's the last time you saw a Fred Dibnah strip-o-gram?

Fred, of course, always was a figure from the past, a man from another age, and it has to be said that in 2016 ladders and ladder men are facing an uncertain future, under threat as much from the health and safety brigade as from the ubiquitous cherry picker.

"Get your foot on the ladder, son" – that's still the advice a father will give his son, just as mine did the day I started looking for a "proper" job.

"But not before you've attended a ladder safety training day, including free blood pressure check, and not without a qualified ladder professional in attendance" – that's what the dads have to say today.

The ladder, of course, is something we are encouraged to climb to achieve success – it embodies the idea that life is uphill all the way. Unless, of course, you do that easiest of very easy things, fall off your ladder and plunge to earth.

Curiously, that is just what happened to a play entitled The Ladder which has gone down in history as the biggest-ever flop on Broadway.

Commissioned by oil magnate Edgar B. Davis, and written by J. Frank Davis, it ran for 794 performances in 1927/28 – J. Frank Davis rewrote it eight times – and lost a staggering $1,255,384.11.

Panned by the critics, audiences were so small that on one occasion the husband of the leading lady walked into the theatre and, assuming that a rehearsal was taking place, marched up to the stage, his dog following behind, and deposited a lunch bag for his wife on the stage by the footlights.

It was a live performance.

Which brings us to another dashing figure from film, stage and television, a popular hero as famed for his ladders as his live performances: Robin Hood, who will insist on wearing his trademark dark green tights while living among the thickets and the thorns of Sherwood Forest.

Robin's got more ladders than the South Wales Fire and Rescue Service. And guess who gets to mend them while Robin's out stealing from the people at the very top of the ladder, or the rich as we sometimes call them. That's right. Poor Maid Marian. It seems the world of the ladder isn't entirely a man's world after all.

Mike Witchell

LEAVES

Only five leaves left: such, in my younger days, was the wording of the small green strip of paper to be found tucked neatly in a packet of Rizlas just before the contents ran out.

Quaint to call cigarette papers leaves, I always thought; it was not a term anybody used, not even the rustic standees in the public bar who coughed and hawked over their "rollies" of Golden Virginia, Old Holborn and Black Beauty.

Leaves <u>were</u> green, true, real leaves – in summer at least - but they adorned trees and plants and hedgerows, while the leaves that once comprised books had long since turned themselves over to become something entirely new known as pages.

Cigarette papers never were leaves, except to the design team at Rizla - they were "papers" if you smoked tobacco, and "skins" if you smoked "something smuggled in", to use a phrase coined by Joni Mitchell.

Leaves of every kind were all around one hot summer's day, far away and long ago, when a friend and I found ourselves marooned for the duration in a very large and very grand garden surrounded by a very large and very grand hedge.

It was our job to prune it.

All that day we toiled, and all the next day, and . . . mysteriously, for every twenty yards we cut, the hedge seemed to take it upon itself to grow thirty yards more. It was apparent that the hedge looked down upon us in more ways than one.
By lunchtime on that third day we had been reduced to praying – for rain, which even in the days before health and safety had been invented, would have precluded further work on the hedge.

Our prayers, alas, went unanswered – or so at least it seemed.

Next morning, however, things started to look up. First the batteries failed which powered the two sets of electric hedge clippers, and when these were replaced by the company mechanic – who took more than an hour to arrive from the yard – we somehow contrived to sever the cables connecting batteries to clippers.

And as if to prove there really is a god of the reluctant gardener, within half an hour both pairs of hand shears had – well – sheared off, the pivot bolt shattered in both cases. It was the end of work for the day.

When we returned early next morning, to our surprise and delight most of the hedge had been cut. Frustrated beyond endurance by our feeble efforts, the property owner – a New Zealand sheep farmer by the name of Horseman – had cut all but a fraction of the rest of the hedge himself.

"Knocked it off after dinner last night," he pointedly informed us. "Only stopped because it got dark."

So there was still a short section left for us to do, and we proceeded to attack it with gusto. As final victory neared, a celebration was clearly in order, Joni Mitchell fashion – and, right on cue, the little green strip appeared in the Rizla packet in my right hand: Only five leaves left.

It was with infinite care and precision that we attached the tiny piece of paper to the miniscule area of hedge that remained uncut. Only five leaves left. We never did discover whether Mr Horseman happened to chance upon it.

Mike Witchell

MANGLE

Funny lot, inventors. Madcap is the go to word
for inventors, to use the modern idiom, and, as
the old saying goes: if the cap fits, wear it.

Take the Dutchman who invented the mangle
back in the sixteenth century. There's Ruud,
holed up in his shed among the tulips, his new
fangled mangle has done its stuff for the very
first time, and he rushes straight into the house
to tell the missus.

"Joyous tidings, Juliana," he says. "I have this day
invented an ingenious new machine to take all
the wrinkles and creases out of my hose and
doublet when you have done washing them."

"An ingenious new machine to take all the
wrinkles and creases out of your hose and
doublet when I have done washing them? Ha!
And with what marketing savvy name, pray, have
you christened your new machine?"

"Mangle it is. Mangle. And mangle will make my fortune by banishing the housewife's washday blues. I'll sell scores of them, you'll see."

"Mangle. Brilliant. You spend years skulking in your shed perfecting a machine to *iron out* wrinkles and creases, and what do you call it? Mangle. Sounds like you're putting them in.

"You couldn't possibly have called it something sexy, something like The Press with the Caress – something that might appeal to the women you expect to use the beastly thing – oh no! You had to call it Mangle. Man-gle.

"And don't think I don't know why. You've always had an unhealthy interest in the, ahem, velar nasal – my mother noticed it at once. You can't say a single sentence without recourse to words like jangle, tangle, wangle and dangle. Obsessed with the n/g sound you are, obsessed."

"We could always try combining . . ."

"There you go again – combin*ing*. Why can't you just say combine? You have to stick the n/g sound on the end, don't you? You and your velar nasal."

"All right, all right! I'll try another angle. Oops. Sorry. Anyway, as I was saying – what am I like? – we could always combine the two names, my love, call the machine Mangle – the press with the caress."

"Oh, it's we now, is it? I see. So you *will* be expecting me to use your so-called mangle. Right, well, while we're talking dirty – dirty laundry, that is - I don't know what you've been doing with that purple codpiece I bought you for your birthday, or who you've been doing it with – I don't want to know – but if it happens again, Ruud - trust me – it's your own precious dangle I'll be putting through the mangle."

All of which nonsense brings me to another sort
of mangle altogether, and a rhyme from the days
when there was a twin tub in every outhouse
and the telly was black and white.

I got mangel wurzels in me garden, I got mangel wurzels in me *shed*,
I got mangel wurzels in me bathroom, and a *mangel wurzel* for an 'ead!

I thank you.

*The *ng sound* is called the "velar nasal," which means you curl your tongue up against the back of our mouth and the air comes out your nose.

**Hancock, The Bowmans, BBC1, 1961.

Mike Witchell

PANTS

Pants the Hart was a firm favourite at the boys' grammar school. Indeed, had the pupils been allowed to choose a school pet, Pants would have romped home almost unopposed.

Choice, though, was something denied them: choice was not in the rules. And the rules covered every aspect of life within school, and some aspects of life without.

Clothing, for example, had to be uniform. The uniform, the whole uniform, and nothing but the uniform – that was the rule, a rule enforced through violence or the threat of violence.

Failure to wear the hated school cap, in the approved position with the peak firmly down over the eyes, would, even for a first offence, mean a visit to the headmaster's study if a boy was unlucky enough to be spotted by certain of the masters or indeed by a smirking prefect – and this, perhaps, on a bus or train some miles from school as the boy made his way to or from.

Visits to the head's study followed a pattern that was uniform in itself. The accused would knock on the door; response there would be none. So he would be forced to wait for up five minutes, his intended humiliation apparent to all who passed by, until finally he received the command "Come".

Once inside, the old man, begowned as always, would greet the boy like a young friend, as if he had no inkling of why the child was there. Confession would invariably follow, as of course the head knew it would - and the mood would immediately darken.

Sin had been committed with the failure to wear the school cap, sin that had brought shame on the boy himself, through his arrogance in thinking to break a school rule; shame on his family, shame on his fellow pupils, and, worst of all, shame on the school of which he was, for now at least, a part.

Eyes flashing with the fire of the Moral Rearmament movement of which he was a leading light, the old man would – with the greatest reluctance, of course – declare himself to be the instrument of God's will, order the sinner to bend over and proceed to chastise him with one of the canes (he had a choice of canes) the Good Lord had provided for the purpose.

Corporal punishment was part of the school tradition, a tradition dating back centuries, just as it was traditional for lessons to be taken not by teachers but by masters; masters who expected to be addressed as "sir" as they had been since time immemorial.

But this was the 1960s, and the times they were a'changin'; deference was being challenged in every way and on every front. During one roll call, for example, a boy answered with the single word "yes" when his name was called. "Yes, what?" said the master. "Yes, I'm here," replied the recalcitrant. Boiling with rage, the master demanded the boy address him as "sir". Said the boy: "'Sir' is a term of respect, and respect has to be earned."

Such direct, individual challenges were rare, however, followed as they inevitably were by the enthusiastic application of cane to seat of pants. Which brings us back to Pants the Hart. Pants, of course, was the creature immortalised in Handel's hymn, As pants the hart for cooling streams when heated in the chase, a favourite of the head master in morning assembly.

It was a firm favourite of the bolshie element – the head master's words -among the fifth and sixth formers too. Throwing off their usual attitude of studied indifference to the whole business of morning prayers and hymn singing, they instead threw themselves into a deafening rendition – not of the hymn as a whole, or even of all the first line. A single word was what they sang, with all the gusto of youth.

"Pants."

You could hear it in the street outside.

Mike Witchell

Printed in Great Britain
by Amazon